To LISA E

WITH BEST

UNTIL THIS SOUL DEPARTS

Jim Puskas

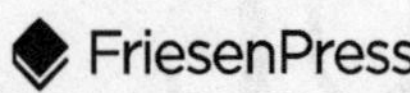

One Printers Way
Altona, MB R0G 0B0
Canada

www.friesenpress.com

First Edition — 2025

Cover art by Samantha Clark.

ISBN
978-1-03-833589-0 (Hardcover)
978-1-03-833588-3 (Paperback)
978-1-03-833590-6 (eBook)

1. FICTION, LITERARY

Distributed to the trade by The Ingram Book Company

Until This Soul Departs is the life story of a man called Teddy McCoy, as told by his resident soul.

The ultimate outsider, Teddy is, by both nature and nurture, an iconoclast. He views mainstream traditions and institutions as impediments to be circumvented. He resents the privileged position of established figures, while at the same time wishing to gain a social foothold in the community that he denigrates. If challenged, his first reaction is to push back aggressively. He embraces his underdog status while striving for personal empowerment.

Teddy's lack of advanced education and social refinement are disadvantages that he strives to neutralize by learning to think more quickly and unconventionally than those he sees as his rivals. Teddy achieves remarkable business and financial success but pays a very high price for it.

The resident soul, intimately aware of Teddy's inner conflicts, seeks to positively influence Teddy on his life journey. But that soul arrives with baggage of its own and also suffers from its own failings.

This story is about Teddy's success, his downfall, and his ultimate redemption. And what becomes of the soul thereafter.

A note about the cover art
by
Samantha Clark
for
"Until This Soul Departs"

Working from the manuscript, Samantha sought to capture some of the character of the protagonist, Teddy McCoy — and his state of mind at a moment in time.

As has been the case throughout most of his life, Teddy is a solitary figure, a man accompanied here only by his dog.

As he strolls along a city street at dusk, Teddy recalls his former life, in the world of development and construction, while he contemplates his current state, and wonders if he still has a future.

"The meeting of two personalities is like the contact of two chemical substances: if there is any reaction, both are transformed."

– G. C. Jung

Time

To begin with, we must understand that
time is cyclical; it has to be.
If that were not so, then time would have
to have a beginning and an end.
But then, what, if anything, could have
happened before time began?
And after time ended, how, where, and
when could anything more occur?

And we also need to know that time encompasses
an untold number of cycles.
They are spinning now and have always been
doing so. Spinning, spinning on…

You and I have been having a ride on
this particular cycle just now.
I've been on many others, so many that I
cannot recall more than a few of them.
It's all become a blur of recollection and forgetfulness.

Every event that we experience, every individual
who is born, lives, and passes on
has existed within any number of time-cycles before,
each of them varied in content, experience, duration, character…

We pass one another.
Flashes.
Voices.
Shadows.
Memories.

We may not pass this way again.
Or perhaps our paths may cross again somewhere. Who can say?

So, please, come along with me for a while.
We have time, you and I. There will always be time.
Let me tell you a story,
one of the endlessly different stories that arise,
pass before the footlights of our consciousness,
and then are gone.
Somewhere.

Selection

A CHOICE MUST BE MADE. And time is so short.

As if time ever runs out!

But run it does, and there's nothing that I can do to modify its progression. The other choices available to me were surely even less appealing than this. And yet I hover, unsure.

There it is, the first shriek. Oh well, at least the brat sounds healthy. But is that the best I can expect, just that the infant isn't sickly? After all my strivings, to be saddled with a mortal whose only worldly asset and excuse for existence is a healthy set of lungs? Have I failed so badly that the best of the choices on offer is this squalling, red-faced newborn whose prospects in life appear to be so bleak?

Fatherless. But then, as it turns out, one might as well say that he was motherless, too!

The glacial fluorescent lights in this antiseptic cubicle that passes for a birthing centre allow for no shadows, no respite from their intrusive and impersonal glare. I ought to sympathize with the resident on duty tonight, stuck here again for the third night in a row, assisting at another nameless birth; it's called paying your dues, the seemingly interminable initiation ritual that you have to survive before they address you as "Doctor" without a smirk. Tonight, he's too exhausted to react to that nurse's sarcastic comments. Right now, his only concern will be about finding his way to a bed, one where there are no pagers and no phones for the next few hours.

I have little reason to sympathize with that young mother, though; her present situation is simply one of the many bits of unpleasantness that she has brought upon herself by her feckless behaviour; so easily distracted by the latest shiny toy, dissolute companion, or momentary sensation. The utter absence of human concern for her welfare in this institutional no man's land at the instant of giving birth? Well, that's just the way things are in any big city. If all goes according to plan, they can send her "home" within thirty-six hours; the administration's only concern will be the validity of her Ontario health card. Tomorrow, the whole sequence will be repeated. Same shit, different day.

But for me, tomorrow will be different. Tomorrow, the inevitable process must begin, the slow, laborious route toward (perhaps) a meeting, a connection, a marrying of body and spirit that is supposed to emerge as a complete being for a time. No point in me worrying about the choice I've made, even less so about the alternative choices I've rejected. My fate is set for the next while; no way of knowing for how long. It has been said that where there is life, there is hope. Perhaps I can help to make this one's life worthwhile.

Act One begins. There is no way to go but onward.

By Way of Introduction

I AM COMPOSING THIS FOR delivery to the world of mortals because it has become apparent that a rare opportunity has arisen, an opportunity to convey knowledge from my existence to yours, and we mustn't miss out. I also have a purely selfish desire to tell you a story; I hope you will forgive me for that. Ordinarily, there are no such lines of communication available and I don't fully understand exactly how this one has come about. Nor does it matter; let's just get on with it, shall we?

To begin with, I should introduce myself. But even that is a challenge. Because, you see, I don't really exist in a way that you are likely to comprehend. I refer here to myself as "I" but there is no "I" as you would perceive a personality or a being. I'm simply applying language that would be relevant to you, even though it's not strictly accurate. No matter. We shall have to do the best we can. Please bear with me for a while.

So, to begin at the beginning, I am a soul. I'm one of a countless number of souls journeying endlessly through time and space (neither of which concepts are particularly meaningful to me, by the way, but it's the best I can do to explain it to you). We souls don't have actual names. We have an entirely different means of recognizing one another, but for the sake of comprehension on your part, I'll call myself Qhd. How you choose to pronounce that is entirely up to you. You see, souls have no voice in a physical sense; sound is meaningless to us because we do not have any material existence. We are only what you would call spirits.

At this juncture (a moment that may occupy an infinitesimally small amount of "time" as you perceive it, or conversely, a seemingly infinite span), I am "between mortals," so to speak. Not presently being occupied with the troublesome business of accompanying a human through his or her brief journey, I am free to work on this little project of offering you and your fellow humans a bit of enlightenment. My most recent host was certainly a vexatious chap, and I found it difficult to steer him away from self-destructive behaviour. A soul's ability to help in these situations is limited; you humans have been given free will, after all. As you may have realized, ours is not a perfect universe. Furthermore, we souls are far from perfect, either; if we were, I daresay things would go a lot better.

Are you still with me? Good! Thank you for not bailing out. I realize that this is a lot for you to swallow. You probably have a host of questions about how all this works. I don't suppose any explanation is likely to be entirely satisfactory, but I'll do the best I can. You're quite free to interpret what I'm about to tell you in any way you see fit. Or you may scoff at the whole thing and refuse to believe any of it. Not to worry. We souls cannot be insulted.

I'll begin by clearing up a common misconception. Those of you who believe in a spiritual reality tend to think of humans (and possibly other sentient beings) as possessing a soul, perhaps an immortal soul. But you see, it doesn't really work that way at all. You do not acquire a soul; a soul acquires you for a time. You might wish to view it as an actor taking on a series of roles; to some degree, the actor is at the mercy of the playwright, the costume designer, the stage manager, and all of whom play a part in establishing the character that this soul is about to portray.

We souls are engaged in an endless journey, migrating from one mortal host to another. We have limited free will in the selection of our next host, our choices being influenced by what has transpired during our most recent host's life—and, indeed, that of a whole series of hosts. What we have endured and accomplished in the past has a complex bearing on the manner in which we acquire our next host.

The physical circumstances that our next host will be born into and the events he or she will face are entirely beyond our control. Having made my limited selection, I have to make the best of it. Don't get me wrong. It's not a punishment/reward sort of thing for us. It's more like an ongoing odyssey, the soul having to endure, toil, seeking to become more complete, more proficient with each successive corporeal episode.

Taking my (rather lame) theatrical analogy a step further, the question surely arises concerning the influence of a director in this particular drama. Take your choice: Do you believe in fate? Or some sort of deity, pulling the strings? Perhaps. But it has always seemed to me that what I've been faced with is a prevailing set of circumstances that are the momentary result of a whole series of interrelated events that have taken place before I stepped onto the stage. What happens next is up to the various players who remain en scène—myself included.

Souls are immortal and do not "age" as humans would envisage it, but we do evolve over time. A soul is likely to pass through any number of cycles of spiritual evolution and devolution, at times becoming more adept at influencing their human host and at other times less so. It may comfort you to know that whether you are adopted by a particularly competent and benign soul or by a soul having shortcomings—or "baggage," as it were—is none of your doing; it's not your fault one way or the other. Your freedom of choice applies only to the mortal aspects of your life.

On the other hand, it's worth noting that a soul associated with a thoroughly corrupt human during its life may become somewhat corroded by the ordeal. Such a soul may not be a very helpful partner for its next host. Worse, a soul that has been accompanying a series of ineffective lives may take a considerable time to get its act together, so to speak. Its current host may, therefore, be lacking in character or robustness of spirit. Such humans do not cope well with physical misfortune or stress; they often exercise poor judgment and have difficulty profiting from experience. They may suffer from psychological or social maladjustment or engage in criminal behaviour. They may be psychopaths or just plain obnoxious jerks. Even if they happen to be blessed with good fortune, they are likely to abuse the privilege.

I suppose you may think that this isn't entirely fair to you: that one of your number should be "saddled," so to speak, with a crummy soul. Well, I have to tell you that we're not happy about the matter, either. But as you may have heard, life isn't fair. Well, sad to say, neither is eternity.

All of you, the living, have contrived to make sense of your existence. Not a trivial undertaking by any means, but one of utmost necessity: denied the solace of meaning, you would all go mad. Many still do. But if I've perhaps raised in you a false hope, that I'm about to answer that eternal question? My apologies—I possess no such wisdom. Each of you, despite your relatively brief existence, has gained just as much understanding as I have during my countless number of life cycles over the centuries.

I'm not about to start any sort of argument with those who buy into Freud's hypothesis of the human psyche, nor those of Jung. Their theories are handy in attempting to explain human tendencies, and they might well have been right. Or not. I doubt if it's that simple. For example, what Freud called the ego might in fact be a collection of unnamed influences, and for all I know, the id and the superego, if they exist, might be operating in another way altogether. As far as I'm concerned, it doesn't really matter.

What does seem to make sense to me is that the human mind is almost always fraught with some degree of internal conflict among the forces of instinct, reality, desire, guilt, and possibly a whole lot of other factors that we may not understand. Where the balance among these forces is struck, or if a balance is ever achieved, depends upon many influences and probably the very fact of human mortality. I won't attempt to sort it out. In my role as the resident soul, I seek to touch and engage all those forces that govern that individual's personality and how they behave. Now and then, I succeed to some extent.

I will only go so far as to suggest that Jung, in his discovery of what he called the *collective unconscious,* might have come close to describing the influence of the soul upon the personality of its host. Jung concluded that the collective unconscious is a reservoir of latent images, values, and tendencies that man inherits from his ancestral past; Jung seemed to see this as a biological process, related to evolution.

Whether he was correct or not, his concept does help me to explain to you the experiences of the soul during its ongoing existence. I have inherited certain spiritual qualities from my past; each of my sojourns with a human host affects me in complex ways. I emerge with psychic benefits from the experiences that that human and I endure together, along with scars from which I may in time recover. And what I have accumulated, for good or ill, is to some degree imposed on my succeeding hosts. The nobility of a virtuous former host may benefit the current one if he is otherwise open to such influences. Regrettably, he will also have to bear some portion of my scars and evil influences.

I know there has been a lot of debate in your world surrounding the matter of the beginning of a human life, notably as it pertains to the vexatious issue of abortion. Let me be clear: opinions concerning human morality, religion, laws, and all of that are none of my concern. I refuse to take sides, and I have enough to look after in my own sphere, the realm of the spirits. As far as I can see, a unique individual human begins forming the instant a sperm penetrates a human ovum and forms a zygote. That embryo is not yet a viable human being, but given favourable circumstances, has the potential to become one. But as I stated at the outset, that human is just a biological living being, a sentient being. It does not possess a soul, but a soul will at some point come to inhabit it. That human is a biological mortal. It lives for a time and then it dies. End of story.

The soul that comes to occupy that body and conscious mind, however, is immortal, has always been immortal, and will remain immortal. It has occupied and influenced an endless succession of human beings, stretching all the way back to the emergence of the first sentient human. If the relationship develops well, the sentient human becomes aware of the presence of the soul. This can (and should) become a harmonious, intimate partnership and the human may come to think of the soul as "belonging" to him or her. But from my perspective, it's essentially the other way around.

Whenever I'm partnered with a living human that I have adopted, I always do my best to develop a relationship with that person's consciousness and influence his or her outlook and behaviour. Within the limits of my own situation and recent experiences (as previously stated, not at all perfect), I seek to be an "angel on your shoulder." The degree to which I can accomplish this is limited by the material I have to work with (that person's psyche), the external influences to which that person is subjected, and the series of events that impact that person's life. It's been said that virtue is its own reward, but I can attest that its achievement is seldom easy.

To be clear: the soul may not come to inhabit that embryo right away at conception; there may be a time lapse, from your perception, viewing time as you do. But any lapse is immaterial. It's essential that the soul take up residence before the embryo develops any awareness of its surroundings and begins to acquire a sense of self. Building a relationship with a human is far from being a simple matter. And I can tell you from experience that it often takes a very long time and a lot of spiritual "shouting" on my part to get that stubborn brute to pay any attention to the soul that is desperately trying to get him to straighten up and fly right. And if that poor soul also happens to be one hampered by its own miserable history of failure? Well, the message is not likely to be very compelling, and the poor bloke doesn't stand much of a chance. Unfortunate, but that's just the way it is.

One encouraging note, for what it's worth: no one can kill a soul. So all the mayhem that is wrought on the earth—wars, massacres, "ethnic cleansing," even the holocaust—all of it consists of crimes against the body of man, not his immortal soul. Such behaviour is simply one aspect of being human. I don't mean to diminish the horror of such things, only to point out their limited impact in the cosmic scheme of things. But at the same time, I can tell you this: the despicable things that humans do to one another and to the world they've been given are extremely painful and troubling to us in the spirit realm. They make our task immeasurably harder, and at times, it becomes almost impossible for us to provide you with any comfort or hope for a better future.

Teddy McCoy

I MIGHT BE ABLE TO tell you a great deal more about how this selection and hosting thing works, and you're sure to have many questions. But I hope that some of your questions will be answered as you read my story. It begins at the point where I was in the process of selecting my most recent host. His name was Teddy McCoy.

Over a vast amount of time, I've been hosted by a great many different humans, many of them becoming brilliantly successful and praiseworthy people. Good people. Important people in their day. But more recently, I have been going through what you might call… a rough patch. My latest few hosts had included, in succession:

- a Southeast Asian warlord, who, while he meant well and tried to improve the overall position of his subjects, had been born into a family of thugs; the only method he understood whereby he could improve his part of the world was by using brute force to govern his clan and subjugate any opponents, either within his own territory or that of neighbouring clans;
- a Mississippi girl raised by a poverty-stricken single mother, who grew up to be a strolling prostitute and was eventually murdered by her pimp;

- a semi-literate day labourer in Liverpool who spent most of his adult life on the dole and amused himself by starting brawls in pubs and at football matches. I must admit to being relieved the night he set me free by plastering his motor bike and bits of himself against a bridge abutment along the Mersey.

None of this qualified me for the choice of a promising host next time around. I had become what you would term a "troubled soul." I had dug myself into quite a hole and would have to earn my way up the scale of available hosts by diligently doing my very best to positively influence each one. That was how I came to land on Teddy. Although his prospects as a human were the best of the short list of newly formed zygotes available to me at that time, all things considered, the outlook was not encouraging. You could say that he had at least one strike against him even before he was born. And he proceeded on a career that appeared hell-bent on making matters worse over the following years. I insist that I did the best I could with him. A brief history of his life and my involvement in it may help you to better understand my situation.

Of course, when I did my first survey of him as a candidate, he wasn't Teddy yet; he wasn't anyone, just a minuscule bundle of cells lodged in a uterus. But travelling about as we do, and having the advantage of a great deal of experience with the troublesome behaviour of the human animal, we souls have access to a more detailed picture than may be obvious to you. There was already quite a lot that I knew about the individual who would become Teddy McCoy. You could say that I went into this project with my eyes open; that is, if I had eyes.

At the moment when that particular sperm made its way to that egg, the young woman who called herself Janet McCoy was entirely unaware of the event; she was in fact oblivious to anything that was going on within and around her, being so stoned that her brain was experiencing nothing much apart from some flashing lights and a vague feeling of levitation. Given her condition that entire day and night, she would also not have been able to identify the source of that sperm. Had she taken the trouble to consider the matter carefully later on, when she was back down to earth and uncomfortably sober, she might have surmised that the donor could have been any one of three or four equally messed-up members of the male persuasion who had wandered in and out of that gathering. Such an investigation, had it taken place at the time, would not have been at all conclusive. And some six weeks later, when Janet finally became aware of her body having omitted another routine but important event—well, by that time, she could not possibly have been able to recall the names or even the faces of any of the men in question.

Such was the inauspicious beginning to the life of that squalling bundle of flesh that first saw the light of day at Toronto's old Wellesley Hospital in 1960. A boy that Janet named Teddy (not Edward or Theodore, mind you) because she had deluded herself into regarding this infant as some sort of cuddly toy. Her first experience with diapers put an end to that fanciful idea, quickly reinforced by the stark realities of sleepless nights filled with infant serenades. Teddy's most notable quality in his early months was a robust voice, capable of notes that would hold their own with a police siren.

I needn't bore you with the depressing details of Janet's lifestyle, other than to tell you that in the light of her helpless situation, one of her aunts offered her a temporary place to stay with her newborn. Her parents, long divorced, had both given up on her years before. Janet had always retreated from any stressful situation by blaming others for her own mistakes and had become hooked on booze and whatever drugs she could get access to, as a refuge from the unpleasantness of daily reality. She had been drifting from one boyfriend to another for several years, any guy who would put up with her sloppy behaviour and provide her with booze and a variety of pills.

During her relatively sober periods, she picked up, and soon lost, any number of casual jobs, but mostly she just mooched on the fellow party-goers she thought of as her friends. It didn't take long for the aunt to reach the limit of her tolerance. The fourth time she found herself stuck for two days with a very irate infant while Janet was away somewhere getting high, the aunt deposited Janet's few belongings at the curbside and delivered one very odoriferous infant to the Children's Aid.

Over the next year or so, the pattern of losing and regaining custody was repeated several times before the infant was placed in foster care. Janet drifted away and her fate has no bearing on our story. I paid her no attention, being greatly preoccupied with finding my way into the consciousness of a somewhat confused and quite bad-tempered toddler. His initial placement was in a relatively stable environment, a large, noisy household occupied from time to time by anywhere from three to six children between the ages of two and ten years.

Teddy had inherited a generous amount of his mother's personality, especially a refusal to abide by house rules, resorting to tantrums or sulking when he didn't get his way. It didn't take long for him to come into conflict with his housemates, and by the time he was starting school, he had become a troublesome handful. For the sake of the other children in that home, most of whom had their own challenges to deal with, an effort was launched to move Teddy elsewhere.

At the age of six, he was placed in a provincially funded boarding school, where he quickly encountered other boys who were just as recalcitrant as he was. A couple of those boys became Teddy's long-time associates. I hesitate to call them gangsters inasmuch as they never became an official "gang" nor could they be termed criminals, having never acquired a police record; or at least none of them were ever convicted of anything. But they certainly were a tough crowd and over the years, they caused a good deal of low-level mayhem in their neighbourhood.

While all of this was taking shape, my task was to establish for myself a position of influence within Teddy's personality and his conscious mind. I must help you to understand the depth and intimacy of this involvement. During a human host's life, the soul cannot escape the full-time reality of its situation. There is no respite; the host is almost entirely outside the soul's control and is subject to all kinds of external influences. When they engage in destructive behaviour, the soul has no choice but to go along for the ride. I had no entity, either mortal or spiritual, that I could call upon for aid or advice. I had to rely on previous experience and was obliged to react to each new challenge.

It's seldom possible for the soul to be proactive. You may suppose that a religious influence or the presence of a devoted parent, teacher, clergyman, scoutmaster, or some such person might be helpful, but that is seldom the case. Too often, the host covertly or even openly objects to such a person, who is perceived as restricting or dominating his life choices, seeking to enforce behaviour, or lay a guilt trip on him. Often, the more closely parents or other authority figures hover, the more they are resented.

I was constantly aware of every thought that crossed Teddy's mind, every scheme he devised to stymie authority—all of his selfish motives, ambitions, resentments, infatuations, and desires. Being constantly in touch with his deepest psyche, I actually came to know Teddy better than he knew himself because I was there in both his waking hours and during sleep, when his subconscious mind held sway. Never try to tell me that dreams are meaningless! I can attest that some of Teddy's most mischievous instincts took centre stage while he was asleep.

The human brain, surely the most complex piece of living matter this world has ever known, has to work very hard, both physically and emotionally. It needs quiet time to flush out toxins, along with emotional waste matter—resentment, anxiety, sorrow, disappointment; the psychic accumulation of unresolved issues that arise out of daily lives fraught with conflict and stress. You need sleep for the repair and restoration of mind and body.

Shakespeare understood this need and expressed it so perfectly: "Sleep that knits up the ravell'd sleave of care…"

Souls, lacking any material limitations, have no physiological need for somnolence. We do not sleep. But I have experienced foolish moments when I have envied all of you, your ability to just turn off and drift away to a refuge free from awareness, leaving your daily cares behind. But then, any such nonsensical idea is quickly scotched by the realization that most of you, even if you manage to sleep soundly, have accumulated so much emotional baggage that your precious mental repose is often hijacked by outrageously stressful (and even violent) dreams. You may wake up physically rested because your body was relatively static, but your emotional hiatus was about as restful as a drug bust in an alley or a heated argument with an irate mother-in-law.

We souls have not been provided with an on-off switch nor even a mute button. One of the several prices we pay for immortality is the denial of repose; we are eternally on duty. So be it.

When a constructive relationship develops between a human's conscious mind and the resident soul, it's a truly wonderful experience. Regrettably, it is seldom attained. The daily life of humans includes far too much noise, too many distractions, too many contradictions. I've never resided with a monk or a mystic; I understand that those souls who have done so found it possible to connect with and profoundly influence their host. In those cases, the host often believes that they are communing with God. If that works for them, all well and good. Far be it from me to enter into any sort of religious debate. I can only state that I've never experienced God, nor have I any opinion to offer about God's existence or role in the affairs of either mankind or the spirit world.

On the other hand, I can assure you that there are instances where a host is at war internally with the resident spirit and that is a terrible thing, a life of unimaginable torture. I've come perilously close to it once and never wish to face it again. In such a case, the host is certain to become insane and the soul may take a very long time to recover, if it ever does.

Teddy's was a very difficult consciousness to reach. He never became a patient, receptive thinker, even in his later life. As a boy, his attention span was brief and haphazard. He craved entertainment, sensation. From an early age, he always looked to others to satisfy his needs, physical or emotional. I found him to be acquisitive, greedy for pleasure, but in a way mentally lazy (more about that later). He was always looking for shortcuts, a way to get what he wanted without undue effort on his part. Like his mother, everything unpleasant that happened to him was someone else's fault. This is not an attractive formula for personal success or peace of mind. Such individuals inevitably encounter conflict and are rarely satisfied with their lives.

To some degree, I believe that Teddy's behaviour along those lines was aggravated by the lack of a loving parent. From the beginning, he saw himself as being alone in the world. He formed few attachments and instinctively adopted selfishness as a survival mechanism. Viewing him as being disadvantaged, I admit to having been overindulgent, willing to forgive him to some degree. But his overall character was not developing in a satisfactory way, and I anticipated a long struggle with scant prospect of success. My primary goals in my relationship with a host have always been peace of mind and peace of soul; the two are separate things but they need to coexist.

You would have to say that I've drawn a quite unattractive picture of Teddy's personality. In doing so, I'm not making excuses for any inability on my part to cope with a difficult assignment; I'll accept full responsibility for any of my own failings. I'm introducing Teddy in this manner because I wish to face reality and explain what was done and why. You may be surprised to learn that I grew to like Teddy despite his shortcomings and to care a great deal about his welfare. The fact that he was unlikely to achieve peace of mind without a great deal of help caused me a lot of concern. I should explain what it was about Teddy that I found attractive.

To begin with, he was highly intelligent, far beyond what was usually perceived by those around him. Surely you can understand that being harnessed, as it were, to a dull, plodding personality for a lifetime would be the least desirable assignment for the soul, a tiresome journey through a colourless landscape of dull mediocrity. There are not likely to be many outright calamities in such a life, but at the end of it all, neither are you left with any satisfying experiences to take forward with you on your next assignment.

Call me selfish, if you wish, but I'm not inclined to invest a lot of spiritual energy in a host who bores me. Teddy had a creative mind, capable at a young age of devising surprisingly subtle and complex strategies to achieve his ends. Those who were exposed to his presence and actions usually came to see him as a schemer and therefore, devious; that was not necessarily a true picture. It was just his nature to think things through. This may appear to contradict what I characterized as mental laziness, but it doesn't, really; Teddy simply sought out the shortest and easiest route to his goals in life. He craved efficiency of effort. If that required him to take the time to devise a better plan, that's what he did.

And yet, whenever Teddy found himself secure and at ease in a situation where he felt no need to defend himself against what he deemed to be a threat, he could reveal a degree of generosity that was quite unexpected. He also instinctively objected to what he saw as unfair advantage being taken of those unable to defend themselves. The people he fought against were invariably those he saw as his equals or rivals. Above all, he resented authority figures. But as a boy, he was usually kind to younger children unless he saw them as being obstacles to him getting his own way. The boys (and later the men) who cursed Teddy's memory were invariably the ones who had underestimated him and sought to outman him in some way.

Above all, Teddy was blessed with a good helping of courage, determination, and the instincts of a survivor, attributes he was certainly going to need. I believed from the outset that Teddy was far from being a hopeless case. That said, over the years, he gave me many opportunities to doubt that assessment. But there's no escape for a soul. Once you're on board, you have no choice but to ride along to the end and help whenever your host will let you.

Perhaps the greatest challenge faced by a soul is finding itself with no means of helping its host to deal effectively with other humans—those people who so frequently create havoc in the consciousness of the host that you're trying so desperately to aid and influence.

Notable are the tempters who lure a person into evil pursuits; the bullies who destroy a person's self-esteem and tranquility of mind; the religious fanatics who fill a person's mind with nonsense and irrational fears; the guilt merchants who victimize a person for their own selfish ends; the overbearing authority figures who rob a person of any sense of self-worth; and the whiners, parasites, and sycophants who waste a person's vitality and distort their perspective. I'll have more to say about all that in the next part of our story.

Surviving Among Humans

IN TEDDY'S EARLY YEARS, WHILE he was still in his first foster home, I began my campaign, beginning with an exploration of Teddy's early personality as he began to develop. I don't necessarily buy into the conventional way that you humans attempt to explain the mysteries of the human mind; whether there's any validity to the elaborate theories that psychologists concoct matters little to me. I find the human mind to be generally chaotic, at its best, and downright perverse, at its worst. I do my best to navigate, probe for points of entry, get to know the loops and pitfalls; above all, I mustn't add to the conflict that's already there any more than necessary. But I never cease sending out signals: "Hey there, chum! You're not as alone as you think you are. I'm available to help, but you've got to figure out how to listen to me!"

It's a discouragingly one-sided conversation: me calling, nobody hearing. I have no voice, so my outreach resembles the futility of one hand clapping. Meanwhile, every human being Teddy encounters has a voice—and some of them make one hell of a racket.

Here's the conundrum I faced: Teddy was, right from the outset, a lousy listener, which means that the human chatter around him rarely penetrated his attention (which was brief, anyway).

Fortunately, his sheer obstinacy helped to limit the damage that would otherwise have been rendered by the vexatious people who surrounded him. Regrettably, he also ignored those people who could have been doing him some good. And because his selective deafness gratified him, it steadily became more profound. He was at risk of not learning from his mistakes. As a result, I was not reaching his consciousness at all. I had to work in the area of his personality that Jung called the *personal unconscious*. Which is not that unusual, in my experience, but my assignment would surely have been a lot easier if I could have reached my host directly.

Sorry to complain. I know you're not likely to be sympathetic to my problems. After all, you would say, I've got immortality working for me.

Teddy's first foster family did the best they could with him, but they had several other troubled youngsters needing their attention; and given the intractable personality they had to work with, they hardly stood a chance. My knowledge of anything physical or medical is based on nothing but hearsay, but I always suspected that Teddy suffered from fetal alcohol syndrome; mind you, he was never diagnosed as such, so what do I know? His state of mind, which I assure you I knew far better than any doctor, led me to believe that some of his tendencies were based on brain chemistry. Anyway, whatever might have been at the root of Teddy's behaviour, those making the decisions about him at the time were in over their heads to begin with, so I'm not blaming them for how things went.

By the time they moved Teddy into that boarding school (in truth, it would have been better described as a junior reformatory, but names don't really matter except for PR purposes, anyway) his pattern of ignoring rules and resenting authority of all kinds had been fairly well established. One thing I will state emphatically: Teddy was no mental weakling. Even trying to reach the unconscious aspect of his mind was very difficult. Boarding school and the boys he met there went a long way toward further reinforcing his strength of mind and his determination to march to the beat of his own drum.

Peter Chumley, the school director (they didn't call him principal) had encountered plenty of boys the likes of Teddy and he did his damnedest to impose his will. Over Teddy's time there, the only positive achievement I could detect was that his survival instinct prompted him to develop what Jung would term his *persona*, a public mask and adaptive behaviour to present the outward appearance of conformance.

That adaptation thankfully kept him from taking actions that would have incurred the severest forms of retribution, the sort of painful experiences that might have turned him into a bitter, resentful young criminal very quickly. Teddy was using his inborn intelligence to figure out how to just get along in a situation that was, from his point of view, overly restraining and not much fun. On balance, I suppose you could say that the school and the staff there did him as much good as they did him harm.

I cannot say the same for the companions he accumulated there. I won't call them friends; Teddy had no obvious use for friends; he instinctively sought out people he could use as allies or from whom he could learn useful skills. And in that learning process, he was exceptionally adept. From those boys, he learned how (and when) to fight, how to deceive adults, and above all, how to convince others in his circle to act in ways that suited Teddy. Right from the start, he was developing the art of dominance—as distinct from leadership, because with Teddy there was never an element of collegiality, shared goals, or mutual advantage. It was always about doing what was good for Teddy's agenda, not necessarily what was best for the group. Teddy accomplished his ascendancy by various means, both overtly physical and subtly strategic.

The process to establish his position among his peers began on his first day, when he was confronted in the schoolyard by a boy named Frank, who was about Teddy's age. But Frank was at least a head taller, confidently aggressive, and accustomed to bullying those around him. Flanked by a couple of his underlings, this boy cornered Teddy and informed him in plain terms exactly who was boss. Being unprepared for such an early encounter and not yet knowing where he stood in an unfamiliar environment, Teddy chose to ignore the challenge; he just turned and walked away.

Not satisfied with such a passive response, Frank grabbed Teddy from behind, twisted his arm, threw him to the ground, and proceeded to administer a quick but effective beating. Teddy reacted in the shrewdest way possible: he took his licking, kept quiet about it, and bided his time. The bully assumed he had won the game.

Two days later, Teddy spotted Frank when his cohorts were out of reach, pounced on the bully from behind, spun him around, and landed a punch right on the nose, followed up with a kick to the groin before he had time to react. The boy doubled up in agony, giving Teddy the chance to bring a knee into hard contact with Frank's chin. Fortunately, young Frank suffered no permanent physical damage, but Teddy spent a couple of very uncomfortable hours in the company of the school director and he discovered how unpleasant it could be to have all privileges suspended for a month. Nevertheless, Teddy's standing among the students had been established from that day forward.

The strategy whereby Teddy dominated his circle centred on making it his business to understand the group dynamics, how the pecking order worked and why, what each player really wanted from the relationship, and, most important of all, what each boy was afraid of. He quickly discovered which boys he could get on his side by feeding their ego, which ones were easily coerced, and how to form alliances to his own advantage. And his quick intelligence, not immediately obvious based on his crude and abrasive behaviour, helped immensely; he simply thought more quickly than most others and got them moving in the direction he wanted before they had time to come up with other plans.

All of that, combined with having subdued the bully who had previously been cock-of-the-walk, soon established Teddy as the boy who set the agenda. He was also prudent enough to limit the scope of his personal fiefdom to one that he could control. He surrounded himself with a small, tight circle of no more than five or six boys at any one time and demanded total loyalty. Those outside his circle he ignored as long as they kept their distance and didn't infringe on his territory.

The group became known among the school population as Teddy's Clan, a name that followed that group long after they had all left the school. Over the years, these same boys, even in their adulthood, never completely lost contact with each other, and repeatedly collaborated in many endeavours, both honourable and otherwise. The Clan was the true beginning of Teddy's remarkable career in life.

The provincial authorities had always intended the placing of boys at that school to be a temporary measure; they sought to place each boy in a more conventional family setting whenever possible. It was understood that an institutional environment was unlikely to produce good outcomes, and in Teddy's case, I'm sure they were eager to separate him from his troublesome associates and get him onto a more controlled and predictable development path.

So when Teddy was twelve years old, he was transferred to another foster home, this time not a group arrangement, but one with only two foster children, the other child placed there being a girl of ten. Mr. and Mrs. Allwood were a puritanical, humourless, implacably religious pair, determined to instill the *fear of God* into the boy. Their house rules were, if anything, even more pervasive and strict than had prevailed at the boarding school. I suppose I understand why that particular household was selected for Teddy, but as it turned out, they had overdone the adjustment.

Teddy was now enrolled in a Christian school of which his new foster parents were founders and directors. At the end of his school day, Teddy was compelled to go directly home, there to be met by Mrs. Allwood, who immediately sat both children down for a half-hour Bible reading, followed by prayers. Mr. Allwood normally arrived at home by the completion of prayers, and both children were then required to give an account of what they had learned in school that day, and to reveal exactly what homework assignments they had been given. They then got started on their homework, which was interrupted only for supper.

After supper, homework had to be completed and reviewed in some detail by the two parents; when that was deemed to have been completed satisfactorily, it was evening prayers and bedtime. On Saturdays, after the week's homework had all been completed, the two children were permitted to spend much of their day at childhood pursuits of a nature that met with the parents' approval. From Teddy's viewpoint, that meant no real choice at all and definitely nothing resembling fun.

Sunday was reserved for Sunday school at 10 o'clock, full church service from noon to 1:30, and quiet reading and contemplation until supper time, followed by bedtime prayers. Any signs of objection on Teddy's part to this egregious regimen were met with long lectures about hell-fire and eternal damnation that awaited young men who persisted in sinful ways. Teddy was provided with extremely colourful descriptions of what tortures Satan would subject him to; I have to admit the man was very convincing and I suppose he really believed all that rot. The lecture was so intense and so relentlessly delivered that it almost succeeded in producing a state of terror in Teddy in spite of his strength of mind. Almost, but not quite.

In the beginning, he was baffled and somewhat awestruck by the man's vehemence. He decided to keep his head down and figure out where the land lay, how the power structure in this bizarre household functioned; for the time being, Teddy was entirely out of his depth, the rules of this new game being foreign to him. The girl who shared this strange household with him was a nonentity, a pathetic little mouse, frightened out of her wits by her overweening, fanatical foster parents. Teddy decided to pretend she didn't exist. He tolerated the regime for two weeks while considering his options.

The breaking point came on a Friday, when it was announced that the entire family would be spending all day both Saturday and Sunday at a religious revival meeting. Teddy had by this time become a human pressure cooker; an explosion was imminent. He calmly declared that he was meeting a group of his pals on Saturday for a softball game and would not be accompanying the rest of the family to the meeting. This was clearly going to be a test of wills. Teddy was abruptly brought to a realization that this was no schoolyard confrontation and that his foster father knew every bit as much about corporal punishment and physical constraint as he did about the Bible.

Teddy had, despite his limited years, endured any number of punishments of varying kinds, but none had ever approached this one in severity and effectiveness. The instrument applied was one that had, in an earlier time, served as a strop for a straight razor: a supple, thick piece of polished leather 2 inches wide and almost 2 feet long. Applied non-stop to the backside with considerable vigour over a five-minute period that felt like a week, it made a lifelong impression on Teddy and rendered it absolutely impossible for him to sit down for many days.

From Teddy's point of view, the apology that was subsequently extracted from him for his disrespectful behaviour was even more galling than the beating he had just endured. It was a valuable lesson Teddy never forgot: make sure of your position before openly challenging a determined authority that has the ability to enforce its decisions. He reconsidered his options and attended the revival meeting; mercifully, no one at that gathering was compelled to sit down.

None of the alternatives facing Teddy were the least bit attractive. Continue to accept and endure the regime? Run away—to God knows where? Sneak into the couple's bedroom in the dead of night with a butcher knife and murder both of them? (Getting just one of them wouldn't do the trick!) Clearly, none of those choices were acceptable. Teddy decided to let his rump heal before taking any further action; launching a serious campaign that could involve vigorous physical activity in his current painful state didn't appeal to him.

I had at that point not yet been able to capture his attention in order to influence his decision; but even had I been able to reach him, I'm afraid I wouldn't have been much help. He continued to endure, but with a firm resolve to escape by some means, in due course. He took advantage of the time to think things through; he determined that his only avenue for a reprieve was to somehow get himself transferred out of that religious fanatic's clutches. To accomplish that would require actions that would no doubt result in some form of punishment far beyond the whipping he had just received, so the risks to his personal well-being were significant.

After several days of deliberation, he decided to burn the house down. That was sure to get him out of there. Probably to jail, but that looked like a far better prospect than what he was currently enduring. The only difficulty he foresaw was how to go about it; specifically, how to get a good blaze under way before anyone caught on. And then, of course, how to make sure to be well out of reach of Mr. Allwood and stay there until the authorities came to arrest him and take him away.

His chance came on a day when both husband and wife were sitting on a bench in the back corner of their garden, reading and discussing Bible passages, as they often did on a Saturday afternoon. Teddy was at the kitchen table, pretending to concentrate on his homework. He wasn't sure where the girl was, but she was out of sight, so she didn't concern him.

From where they sat, the Allwoods could not see what was happening inside the house. Teddy quietly slipped out the front door, around the side of the house, and into the garage, where he retrieved a small canister of gasoline that was kept there for the lawnmower. He silently retraced his steps, through the front door and into the living room, where he emptied most of the gasoline onto the curtains, rug, and furniture, the last dribble forming a trail through the kitchen, along the hall, and to the front door. He had planned this carefully, having several matches at the ready in case the first one didn't catch the gasoline.

He needn't have worried about that; within seconds, the flames raced half the length of the house. Only then did he hear the girl calling from the bathroom about smelling smoke. There was no time to lose. Teddy dashed out the front door and away down the street as fast as his legs could carry him; he made it all the way to the nearest police station to turn himself in without ever hearing the sirens of the fire department vehicles rushing to the scene.

You may wonder what I was about while all this was happening. But you see, there wasn't anything I could do about it; the actions of mankind are outside our control. Once emotion takes over, we souls can only observe events and try to exert a better influence next time. It's always the same. We watch you start wars, invent new religions, destroy vast areas of your little planet, and all the while, we're seeking subtle ways to at least modify your ruinous behaviour. I'm pleased to report that the little girl, now even more terrified than ever, escaped otherwise unharmed. By the time the firemen arrived and got the flames under control, there was very little salvageable of the house or its contents.

Teddy was sent to a real juvenile detention centre this time; no pretensions of it being a school. His career as a delinquent was off to a roaring start. To his immense relief, he never encountered the

Allwoods again; had he done so, in the absence of some third party to exercise restraint, I suspect my term of duty with Teddy McCoy might have ended abruptly due to Teddy's untimely demise.

Growing Up Fast

ASSIGNMENT OF A CHILD TO juvenile detention centre was a court-ordered event. It was not just a simple matter of transfer of custody. The assessment process and its outcome were made known to Teddy by way of a bewildering sequence of meetings and interviews rather than any attempt to inform him about it in person. No one ever explained anything to Teddy about what was to be done with him. All those decisions took place elsewhere, to make sure the one person most directly concerned with it all would know nothing about it, and would most emphatically have no say in the matter.

Teddy had every reason to expect dire consequences from his desperate act. That's the nature of desperate acts, isn't it? They are taken under circumstances that provide for few, if any, convenient options. So the events that took place after he was taken into custody were probably no worse than he had anticipated. A pleasant outcome was not expected. He had made a conscious choice to extract himself from an intolerable situation, regardless of the cost.

What did, in fact, transpire was a scenario that he could not have anticipated. It began with what were, to him, a series of very strange conversations. Those interviews alternated between sessions where the object of the exercise seemed to have something to do with gathering evidence whereby he could be condemned to some as yet undefined punishment—and very different sessions that sought to probe into his past experiences, his fears, his imagination, his personal desires, and his ambitions (which implied evil influences and intent).

The former sort of interviews Teddy regarded as routine and normal; they concerned him not at all. His previous experiences had taught him a simple principle: you transgress and there's going to be punishment. Unpleasant, but unavoidable and easy to understand. The latter kind of scenario, however, scared the hell out of Teddy.

Those interviews were conducted by people who seemed innocuous enough on the surface, even sympathetic; but their manner put Teddy on full alert right from the get-go. These people—first a middle-aged woman who spoke very gently, like a fakir attempting to mesmerize a snake, followed by a strange-looking old man with a lisp who was undoubtedly a mad scientist or a con artist—avoided accusing Teddy of any wrongdoing. They asked peculiar questions that seemed to have nothing to do with Teddy having set fire to that house but rather appeared aimed at getting Teddy to confess to some other unnamed sins of far greater significance, some dark, personal secrets, evil impulses, shameful acts for which he could be facing truly horrendous consequences.

The possibility of a death sentence did not enter his mind; that is, until the matter of his intentions regarding the little girl were explored. Did he know that she was still in the house when he set the fire? Why did he hate her? Was it because of something some other woman or girl had done to him at some time? Did he dream about women or girls? What did he remember about his mother, and did he resent not having a father? The fact that Teddy had no answers to most of these questions made him realize that there was no hope for him; he had long ago learned that to escape or even to reduce punishment, you must have a good story, a plausible excuse, or someone else upon whom to throw suspicion or blame.

No child can possibly hope to hold his own against the subtle skills of a trained psychoanalyst. Teddy almost began to regret having taken the actions he had. But as the interviews continued and the process itself struck him as a devious form of punishment with no discernible conclusion, Teddy's inborn strength of mind began to assert itself. He did what had always been instinctive for him: he rebelled. His fear was gradually replaced by anger. Let these creepy people do whatever they wished. He would not be terrorized by them!

He made up his mind to bring this whole process to a conclusion; when he was asked point blank whether he had intended to kill the little girl in the fire, he declared that indeed that had been his intent. That had a very satisfying effect, causing the interviewer to catch her breath, pause, and look over her notes. She seemed confused. Now Teddy had her on the defensive. From that point on, the conversation took on an entirely different character. The woman seemed nervous, unsure of her next question. A valuable lesson had been learned: the people asking questions are afraid of what answers you might give. These people are a bunch of phonies! They have no idea how to deal with a Teddy McCoy. Just feed them a line of horseshit, and they'll run away and leave you alone.

There was nothing that I could do to help while all this was going on. I saw that Teddy, through sheer stubbornness, was likely to come through it alright, but there were sure to be unfortunate longer-term consequences. From the nature of the interviews, I could discern that there must have been a strenuous argument going on between the police and juvenile control authorities on one side and the child psychologists on the other. The issue was whether Teddy McCoy was just a confused, frightened kid with emotional problems, or a vicious, vengeful young psychopath intent on simply raising as much hell as possible for his own gratification.

Faced with Teddy's most recent actions and his previous history, and reinforced by his defiant responses to questioning, there was no doubt about the conclusion that would be reached, This was a youngster who would have to be confined, closely supervised, and treated as potentially dangerous. The director of the juvenile detention centre, having been provided with a comprehensive profile, recognized that in Teddy McCoy he had just inherited a problem, a troublemaker of the first order; and he vowed to make sure that any time young Mr. McCoy chose to step out of line, he would be dealt with appropriately.

Teddy entered the juvenile centre in a defiant and reckless state of mind, resentful toward what were, from his perspective, nameless, arbitrary, and hostile authorities intent on ruining his life. Emotionally, he was on a constant slow boil, liable to erupt in unpredictable ways at the slightest provocation and oblivious to any consequences. But he was soon made to understand that any such outburst was certain to be detrimental to his welfare; no disobedience or defiance would be tolerated.

What he was in desperate need of was a period of tranquility, where nothing of importance to him was taking place; a quiet time wherein he could regain his equilibrium and not feel that he was under constant attack. He slept fitfully, brought to instant wakefulness at the slightest noise. He was beset by episodes of panic when awake; strenuous, violent dreams when asleep.

How can I convey to you my experience of being a largely powerless observer of Teddy's dreams? Fully conscious of the unreal, irrelevant, and pointless existence of the dramas they spun in Teddy's subconscious mind, I was nevertheless swept along with whatever mad adventure was afoot, myself unable to escape into either wakefulness or oblivion. Avalanches of unseen, unstoppable forces thundered upon, over, into, and through Teddy's perception of himself. And whatever it was that was assaulting him would fling him out of one horrid unreality into yet another that was beyond imagining.

On the other hand, Teddy was not always helpless, at the mercy of these hobgoblins; as often as not, his truculent nature asserted itself and he exacted his own share of violence upon his demons. In dreams, as in his waking existence, Teddy was beset by enemies, but he never succumbed to those forces. Teddy McCoy would not become a victim!

The only helpful measure I had at my disposal was to begin introducing scenes of peaceful reassurance into his dreams, experiences of leisure and harmless play. Over a period of several weeks, his sleep began to improve and I like to think that my intervention had been beneficial. But I believe it was the sheer uneventfulness of his new life that had the most calming influence. Stultifying as it was, the rigidly imposed routine that surrounded him was, in fact, just what he needed at that point in his young life; an environment where all decisions concerning him were out of his hands, where there was nothing that he could or needed to do to influence his fate.

Despite such a rocky beginning, his own resilience saw him through the transition to life in that institution, where he was to reside for the next four years. His initial episodes of rebellion were swiftly and effectively addressed by a staff that was well versed in dealing with recalcitrant youngsters of all kinds. The rules, both written and otherwise, were harsh; either you made the adjustment and learned how to march to the same drumbeat as everyone else, or your daily life would quickly become a great deal more unpleasant.

It was immediately apparent to Teddy that he was being monitored very closely. For the first month, his interactions with other residents were kept to a minimum. A full review of his behaviour was conducted at the end of each week. Recognizing that he was being judged more harshly than his peers, he developed a personal hatred of the director, but soon learned that defying the man was futile and counterproductive. His punishments for even the most trivial infractions were as severe as the institutional rules allowed. He was angry and resentful, but determined to hold his own and rise above every obstacle placed in his way.

To avoid the frequent and severe reprisals that he faced whenever he broke any rule, he learned to cover his actions and plan his exploits carefully. He was so deeply engaged in what he understood to be a contest of wills—a contest he came to relish—that I found it impossible to reach him, to influence him in any way at all. Whatever life journey Teddy McCoy was about to pursue, I would just have to hang on and suffer through it with him. The personal style that would characterize Teddy McCoy throughout his life had been set.

He soon became acquainted with fellows his age who had already acquired many of the skills that are useful in a life of hell-raising and petty crime. His real turning point came when two of the boys who had been part of his Clan at school also arrived on the scene. From that nucleus, the Clan was soon well established again, and Teddy knew that better days were in sight for him. At the end of his first two years of incarceration, having finally demonstrated what was deemed to be a pattern of acceptable behaviour, Teddy and others like him were able to obtain day passes on Sundays to explore the neighbourhood, at first accompanied by a minder who monitored their activity. Six months along, if all went well, the minder could be withdrawn.

Amid stirrings of puberty, entire new vistas began opening up in Teddy's life—wondrous, outrageous lies muttered under the bleachers at a local schoolyard on sultry summer afternoons; late-night discussions with his bunkmates; authoritative accounts of the mysteries of girls' bodies, only the most unlikely ones given any credence. Who knows, perhaps if I had been able to conjure up for Teddy images of half-seen bellies, new-formed breasts, or fumblings in the dark on improbable adventures, I might have been able to capture his attention, turn his mental glance my way more often. But of course, I did nothing of the sort, and Teddy continued on his chosen path.

The most important thing he had to bear in mind was to make sure the minder was well out of the way any time he met up with a girl. The directives given to the minders were quite clear on that score: "Make damn sure that these rascals don't mess about with the local kids—specifically the local girls." Parents in the neighbourhood were quite particular about with whom their daughters came into contact. The presence of the juvenile centre in their part of town was barely tolerated to begin with. It would take only one unfortunate incident, some otherwise blameless girl getting "messed up" by one of these delinquents, who were "being allowed to run loose around town, getting into God knows what sort of deviltry," and all hell would break loose.

The centre had enough problems to deal with, just keeping their charges in line, without having to face a mob of half-hysterical mothers and fathers demanding answers and action. The political and PR aspects of this matter were not explained to the boys; it was put to them in much simpler terms: "The first time we spot you even looking the wrong way at some girl out there, you will be grounded permanently until the day you waltz out of this joint free—if you should be lucky enough for that to ever happen."

Which, naturally, ensured that each boy, to gain any sort of personal credibility, would do his damnedest to find ways to encounter girls and acquire convincing evidence of having done so. All the while keeping the minder and his boss in blissful ignorance of his exploits.

In the midst of such life-affirming matters, the pathetic nudges emanating from a boy's soul, regardless of how persistent, were unlikely to gain much attention. In the mind of a fourteen-year-old Teddy McCoy and others like him, sex pretty much fell into the same category as social status, money, and goals scored on the soccer pitch: things to strive for, and if attained, to be able to brag about. It was mostly just the numbers that counted. In Teddy's mind, any of the girls he succeeded in getting his hands on were markers on a personal score sheet. This, too, became part of what made Teddy into the sort of man he became.

Whenever Teddy found himself at large, he used the opportunity to begin establishing local contacts outside of the institution and preparing for his future career, being very careful not to get caught in any mischief. Even though he had adapted well to the juvenile centre, a place where he understood the rules and had learned to tolerate them—at least most of the time—he wished not to jeopardize his scheduled release. He looked forward to a far more interesting life and the freedom to live it in his own style.

Even in the case of a model student—which Teddy certainly was not—at the age of sixteen, it would become impossible to place a boy with another foster home; upon release from juvenile detention, Teddy was shifted to a halfway house, where he was more or less free to come and go as he pleased as long as he was back inside by curfew—and, above all, stayed out of trouble.

His Clan, now having morphed into a group of juveniles running errands for a couple of local street gangs, had become a well-established presence in the neighbourhood, pulling off the occasional smash-and-grab, victimizing street vendors, hot-wiring the occasional car for a joy ride, or snatching a purse or two from unsuspecting tourists. They had become so cunning in their exploits that they never actually got caught, even though they were constantly under suspicion. They had become so accustomed to being picked up by the police for questioning that they appeared to be bored with the routine and knew every local cop on a first-name basis.

At eighteen, Teddy was released from the group home, by which time he had almost but not quite completed grade eleven.

Although his formal education was scanty, he was nobody's fool; having no illusions about his situation or his immediate prospects, he resolved to find a real business for himself: petty crime held no future—it paid poorly and he was sure to get caught sooner or later.

Through the experience of being thrown out of a number of local bars, youth centres, and poolrooms on several occasions, he became aware of the demand for low-cost and somewhat informal muscle at such establishments. The same thing held true at rock concerts, company picnics, soccer matches, and so on. The organizers of events, and managers of small businesses were reluctant to hire licensed security companies; their cost could be prohibitive. They couldn't resort to biker gangs to provide security because their presence only attracted the cops and often led to more trouble than they were worth, not to mention the bad public image of obese, unshaven bikers hanging about.

Several of Teddy's Clan members were of a physical size that offered the requisite degree of intimidation to make them at least appear to be useful as bouncers or gatekeepers. As their leader, Teddy, in effect, became a labour contractor and soon established a fairly regular and diverse clientele that regarded him and his entourage as little more than a band of punks; affordable and handy when needed, but not to be taken seriously. Teddy swallowed their disdain, kept his crew in line, maintained a low profile, and vowed to make them all take him seriously before long.

Several of his clients were small builders who required guards at construction sites in off-hours to prevent theft of equipment and building supplies—especially electrical and plumbing stuff, the sort of materials that could easily be converted into cash. To land those jobs, Teddy and his Clan had to go some lengths to establish their bona fides. Meaning that they all had to keep their noses absolutely clean. Teddy let it be known that anyone in the Clan who continued to indulge in petty theft, no matter how small, would be kicked out of the Clan and reported to the police. He only had to make good on that threat once, and there was no such problem with his entourage thereafter.

The business dilemma he faced was that his crew's objective was to make sure nothing in the way of trouble took place while they were on the job. So when they succeeded, no one noticed their presence or the value of their efforts; any problem that arose would be viewed as a failure on their part to do their job effectively. This was, perhaps, an enterprise not ideally suited to one with as little patience as Teddy.

Resentful of the high wages earned by unionized workers in the building trades, compared to his own small earnings, Teddy developed a strong prejudice against unions, which helped to improve his relationship with some of their employers. On a couple of occasions, his Clan served as security to escort strike-breakers crossing picket lines. That kind of job was high-stress work that sometimes involved a degree of violence that Teddy preferred to avoid; but it paid much better than their usual fees. And it was an assignment that got him noticed—on both sides of the picket line.

In the course of one such venture, he developed an especially cordial relationship with two local non-union contractors. One of those small companies, called Alpha Béton, was a loose partnership of three roughnecks originally from St-Léonard Quebec; there they had run up against a local gang even tougher than they were and decided it was in their best interests to relocate to Toronto. They specialized in excavation, formwork, and foundations, but would take on anything as long as it called for concrete. The other company, operated by two brothers, Gino and Alberto Belacci, provided paving, general masonry, and stonework.

Having always had to watch his back and look after his own interests, Teddy developed excellent powers of observation. Poorly educated and unsophisticated as he was, he was quickly developing into a crafty and creative strategic thinker. Unlike most of his peers of similar background, he taught himself the value of delayed gratification. Despite making more money than most young men with such modest qualifications, he didn't spend extravagantly; he began to accumulate savings, which he put to good use in ways that enabled him to develop a bit of capital. He had discerned early on that the life of a hireling offered relative freedom from stress and entailed limited accountability for outcomes; you got paid when the job was done, and you went on your way, with no strings attached.

But the guys who ended up holding onto most of the money were the ones who owned the business and wrote the cheques. Money passed through their hands and somehow part of that money stuck to them along the way. Success in that kind of endeavour appeared to depend on how the deal was structured, as well as who you knew and who got paid off to keep his mouth shut. He also grew to understand that those who were getting paid off were also on the hook to the guys who had paid them off. Once on the take, it was almost impossible to be your own man again. Teddy made up his mind to find ways to be one of the men with sticky hands, but not one of those who owed their continued survival to someone else's willingness to keep a secret in return for favours.

While Teddy and his crew continued providing valuable services to both Alpha Béton and the Belacci brothers, he watched for an opportunity to obtain a piece of the action, an ownership role that he could build upon. Having made his small enterprise increasingly useful to his clients, each time he was engaged by them, he began to raise his fees, reaching a level that caused his clients to begin looking for ways to cut the cost of security; but not high enough to set them off on a determined search for a different service provider.

In 1981, when the two companies decided to merge their businesses, Teddy saw his opportunity. Having set the scene by creating a measure of price discomfort in his clients, he made them an offer that would reduce their cash outlay for his services, stabilize their relationship, and make him and his crew financially accountable for business results.

In return for a fairly modest payment up front, he was allowed to buy in as a silent partner, his official role being to provide security, but his real purpose being to keep eyes and ears on work sites and the local bars, poolrooms, and other places where workers hung out, to smell out union-organizing activity. With Teddy fully on board, the partnership became very adept at spotting outside union organizers, who would appear from time to time, and taking steps to discourage them from hanging around. He learned how to identify workers who were likely to stir up trouble from within the ranks, and helped the contractor remove them quietly, by one means or another.

Far from being satisfied with his initial role in the business, Teddy and his crew also began applying their surveillance and information-gathering skills in other ways: finding out what new contracts might soon come up for bidding, who the real decision makers were, who might be open to influence by a few favours, and even who in the public sector might have guilty secrets that could be used as leverage.

Over my centuries of accompanying a numerous and diverse assortment of hosts through their lives, it's been rare that any of them progressed as far in their chosen field after having been given as few advantages up front as did Teddy McCoy. Here was an orphaned kid with scant education, no family connections, and absolutely no hard knowledge in the building trades; and yet, at less than twenty-three years of age, he had made himself junior partner in a fair-sized general contracting company. What Teddy lacked in experience, mechanical skills, and construction business know-how, he more than made up for through his understanding of people, their weaknesses, and especially their behaviour under stress. He instinctively understood how to operate within the darker sides of human nature.

And I saw a pattern emerging in Teddy that was likely to provide my young, ambitious host with some early successes but would also entail significant risk over the long term.

Making a Noise

OVER THE FOLLOWING COUPLE OF years, three more small contractors joined the consortium, broadening their scope to include everything from steel frame construction, tile, and terrazzo, to glass, roofing, and even electrical work. The first real breakthrough came when Duff Simon and his son Jack agreed to bring their family-owned steel construction company into the partnership. The Simon family were Mohawk, originally from Kahnawake; that made them royalty, as far as the high steel trade was concerned. Putting up high steel used to be a tradition handed down through generations among the Mohawks. They became known and revered all over North America.

It had all started way back in the 1880s, when Dominion Bridge was building a bridge over the St Lawrence River from New York State into Quebec, crossing over the Mohawk reservation at Kahnawake. Young daredevil Mohawks were spotted climbing the steel just for fun and it occurred to some Dominion Bridge people that some of these young men might be trainable as ironworkers; the rest is history. Over the past hundred years, Mohawks have had a legendary role in erecting almost every major skyscraper and high steel bridge in North America.

In the early 1970s, Duff Simon became the first Mohawk to break the barriers, establishing his own ironwork company as a business owner and independent contractor instead of working for hourly wages, as his father and his grandfather before him had done. By the beginning of the 1980s, the economy was changing, and it became less attractive for Kahnawake men to make the trek to New York City and elsewhere. Work on high steel had its own glamour and mystique and paid well, but living costs in the big city were high. Meanwhile, conditions back on the reserve were changing, too, and the high-risk itinerant life of an ironworker became less attractive. The Simon family had made the transition from tradesmen to business owners at the right time.

When Teddy McCoy first met Jack Simon, a man five years younger than himself, he sensed a less than comfortable kinship with this brash young Mohawk; Jack had faced prejudice all his life, except when he was several hundred feet above ground with nothing but an 8-inch-wide steel flange between himself and a quick death. Up there, the only pedigree that counted was whether you knew what the hell you were doing.

Despite a century of ironwork by him and his forebears, his father had fought a long battle to gain acceptance as the owner of a business. Jack's mother was of the Curotte family, ironworkers through two generations; she was born on the St. Regis Reserve, which, like Kahnawake, sits on the US–Canada border. Because her family lived on a part of the reserve that the USA considered to be US territory, she was deemed by the US government to be a US citizen (albeit lacking in some of the rights normally accorded to one such).

Young Jack, intensely aware of his heritage, refused to consider himself either American or Canadian; he counted himself a member of the Mohawk Nation. His father, having had his personal aspirations tempered by a lifetime spent finding his way through the maze of aboriginal relationships with national governments and bureaucracies, didn't concern himself with such matters, and focused his mind on running a business. For him, "the only difference between Americans and Canadians is the colour of their money." His priority was seeing to it that money of both colours found its way into his company's accounts.

Jack's father had sent his son aloft on his sixteenth birthday. Jack candidly admitted that it had taken two stiff drinks and the risk of his father's scorn to get him up there that first day and he had to change his underwear as soon as he got back down. The fear never totally left him; he just learned how to manage it. To outward appearances, he was utterly calm and at ease walking an 8-inch beam hundreds of feet up with nothing but fresh air to grab onto, but he insisted that if you lose respect for the realities of the job, you're in trouble. Accidents at those heights are never trivial.

So Jack Simon had learned the ironworker's trade from the ground up and literally all the way to the top. Along the way, his father had also taught him the business side of ironwork. Neither he nor his father could be pushed into committing to something they couldn't complete; and their bid numbers were based on reality. The Simons' personal history and aboriginal credentials enabled them to attract the most skilful and reliable ironworkers from among the dwindling ranks of Mohawks who still pursued the trade.

They had always operated as subcontractors to whatever prime contractor ran the show, but as a full partner of this newly established organization, they found themselves, for the first time, having a say in bidding on major jobs. From the other partners' perspective, bringing a Mohawk steel construction firm into the fold offered the firm a degree of credibility that they probably didn't really merit. Just because you are able to erect high steel and keep it from falling down doesn't necessarily mean that you have any business acting as sole contractor on high-rise construction, unless you possess all the other organizational attributes for carrying out complex projects, and the integrity to go with it. Nevertheless, it was, on balance, an advantageous relationship on both sides.

Teddy soon found that dealing with Jack Simon and his taciturn, no-nonsense father was an entirely different matter from the sort of give-and-take affair that he had established with the original partners. Duff Simon proved to be stubborn, sticking to his own self-imposed rules and standards. Teddy and his other partners tended to regard rules and standards as guidelines—targets to be aimed for rather than operational boundaries. For them, any available shortcut that would save them time, money, or both was worth considering.

And yet, even though that rigidity at times caused Teddy a lot of grief, he eventually came around to taking Duff Simon's side when they strongly disagreed with the other partners on a matter of workmanship standards and safety because Duff had a predictable argument to present: "If you're that sure of your position in the matter, I expect you to accompany my guys up there while the work is being done and trust your lives to the connections being made. And after that, you can join my crew for lunch under that structure the first day that the wind is blowing so damn hard that the crane operator refuses to climb up to the cab."

Neither Teddy nor any of his partners were inclined to take Duff up on that offer, so he usually got his way. Teddy bought in to Duff's point of view because he presented his case man to man instead of acting as some kind of authority. Over the years, imposed rules had often triggered an instinctive push-back on Teddy's part. Logic and the guts to back up your position appealed to Teddy. This was useful information for me to retain in my future efforts to influence his behaviour.

Teddy McCoy was, from the beginning, a lot more competent at playing the contracting game than he was at delivering on what he undertook to do. Such shortcomings rarely troubled him or his partners. They were too busy getting rich to concern themselves very much about the real value of what they were building.

They had become accustomed to regarding themselves as successful entrepreneurs; and to be fair, in the midst of a building boom, they were competing against a few other firms that could scarcely be considered any better. The overall standards of skill, competence, and trustworthiness in the construction industry left much to be desired. Often, the unfortunate client they served only began to realize the fundamental deficiencies of the contractor when the project fell behind schedule, or ran over budget. The true measure of the contractor's mettle was usually to be found in the length and seriousness of the deficiency list they were left to haggle over when the project was officially completed.

Once the Horton brothers, a small heating, ventilation and air conditioning outfit became part of the consortium, the partners began to think of themselves as true general contractors—although they were in fact still little more than a group of roughnecks who had elbowed their way into the front ranks of the building industry largely through bluff, bravado, and some aggressive cost-cutting measures. They named the newly completed partnership STB Contractors; when anyone inquired as to what that meant, they said it stood for "simply the best." Among themselves, they acknowledged that it actually meant "screw the bastards!"

The expanded firm was doing very well, pulling in sizable contracts and stickhandling their way around confrontations with the construction trade unions, something that had become increasingly difficult ever since the passing of significant new labour legislation in Ontario in 1979. They ran non-union crews when it was possible to do so; otherwise, they found creative ways to buy off union organizers who could be bribed; and occasionally resorting to strong-arm tactics in dealing with militants. Although Teddy's hard knowledge and skills in the building trades were almost nonexistent, his skill in smelling out opportunity and negotiating an advantageous agreement made him an increasingly important member of the organization; and as the business grew, his role expanded along with it.

Despite Teddy's most creative schemes, he and his partners were effectively excluded from municipal jobs, the city not wishing to run afoul of its own unions. But they were often able to get around that by acting as subcontractor to play catch-up when the prime contractors fell behind on their schedule. In such cases, the city would usually allow a non-union subcontractor to be engaged for brief periods.

Teddy's brashness went some way toward enabling him to succeed in actions that no one at his stage of life should have been able to get away with. He bluffed his way into negotiations, where he and his partners came nowhere close to meeting the qualifications as a serious bidder. He talked a good game and usually managed to deliver results that could not have been expected, given the resources he had at his disposal. Inevitably, he got in over his head at times, placing his shaky partnership in a contractual bind from which they could not escape without serious consequences.

Hungry for new business, at Teddy's insistence, they bid low enough to land a contract that included, among other things the entire plumbing, heating, and air conditioning systems in an office tower, an undertaking that was far beyond the capability of the Horton brothers, who handled the mechanical work within their consortium. Within four months, the installation work was six weeks behind schedule, causing a major progress payment to be withheld. That left the entire partnership in a cash flow shortfall; unable to pay their supplier of plumbing fixtures on time, they were denied further credit, leaving them critically short of supplies, and unable to proceed with the work.

By any reasonable code of behaviour, Teddy's performance in that matter was inexcusable, the reckless acts of an amateur. Had he been engaged with a conventional contractor that played by the rules, Teddy would no doubt have been unceremoniously turfed out of the partnership, and that might well have been the end of his audacious career. Moreover, I understand there were some companies engaged in that line of work where Teddy would not have been permitted to walk out the door with his entire anatomy intact. He was fortunate that the people he was in business with were cut out of very much the same cloth as Teddy himself; all of them had made similar mistakes themselves when they overreached or simply lied about what they had to offer and got caught short.

After making Teddy sweat for a few days, uncertain of what sort of retribution would be meted out to him, the partners put their heads together, and having decided to go all in, obtained outrageously usurious short term financing from a loan shark, enabling them to pay for the needed supplies and bring an outside mechanical subcontractor on board to get them back on schedule and finish the job.

Remarkably, all the while this was going on, Teddy never missed a sound night's sleep. Despite the very real possibility of being kicked out of the consortium, or of the entire business failing altogether, he never panicked. He simply focused his mind and his energies on working out a solution; he even managed to negotiate a small reduction in the loan shark's exorbitant interest rate, a feat that none of his partners had believed possible. Even though he had got them into the fiasco to begin with, he was roundly congratulated for pulling it off. I began to realize what a brilliant and ruthless strategist I had found myself bound up with.

Even though they had recovered in the end, by falling badly behind schedule for a time, they had impeded the work of other major contractors on the site and were threatened with penalties. The Horton brothers, who, as partners in the consortium, had been placed (by Teddy) in a position where they were bound to fail, were saddled with the loss of reputation. The other partners blamed the whole episode on the Hortons and, in short order, bought them out of the partnership at a deep discount, leaving the Horton brothers essentially broke and out of business.

Teddy further redeemed himself by convincing the very group that they had engaged as mechanical subcontractor to join the partnership, a major upgrade to the consortium's overall capability. The Horton brothers lost out through no fault of their own, the consortium ended up stronger than before, and Teddy, the artful dodger, escaped unscathed. The only members of the consortium who never bought into the exoneration of Teddy were Duff and Jack Simon, who saw the entire experience for what it was: evidence of a deeply flawed and unscrupulous way of doing business.

Through all the years of their partnership, until the day that Duff Simon retired and turned his share of the enterprise over to Jack, he would refuse to sign off on any proposal authored by Teddy without personally verifying all the numbers that affected the steel framing part of the bid. Teddy and Jack, being closer in age and having some personality traits in common, eventually learned to get along, but Jack never grew to trust Teddy's judgment, a fact that rankled with Teddy. In due course, events were to prove that Jack's reservations were justified, but by then it would be too late for Jack's influence to save the day.

I don't pretend to understand much of the complexities of business, but it became obvious to me that my host was engaged in a line of business where fairness was nonexistent, and that it was an environment for which Teddy McCoy was admirably suited. I found myself increasingly impressed by a host that I was liking less every day. I foresaw a long and perhaps fruitless struggle to instill in him anything resembling a code of honour. This angel on his shoulder was finding its wings decidedly ineffectual. Based on my lengthy experience, I also knew that sooner or later, Teddy's luck would desert him, no matter how clever he believed himself to be. There would come a day when he would crash and burn and I would be very regretfully present at his downfall.

As Teddy carried on in his aggressive style, I was compelled to engage in a lengthy review of a great many of my previous engagements, searching for inspiration, ideas that had worked before, hosts who had embarked on similar modes of living and had turned their lives around. Had my influence been a critical element in their success? If so, what qualities had I been able to discover in those hosts that I was able to harness for good? If I had succeeded before, surely I could do so again. Perhaps I would be able to use previous experiences to gain some traction with this stubborn, impetuous young man whose early life had rendered him so hell-bent on getting his own way, regardless of the cost.

In addition to examining my host's qualities, his character, and his habits that I had got to know very thoroughly, I knew that it was vital for me to understand his motivation for every action that he took, even if he himself lacked a deep awareness of what it was that drove him. In some ways, Teddy's actions often appeared to be contradictory. For example, he had always been deeply loyal to his immediate partners at each stage in his young life. And yet, in this latest episode, he had wantonly jeopardized the financial and reputational welfare of his organization by overcommitting them to a contract that he must have known they lacked the resources to fulfill.

Had I overestimated his sense of obligation to his partners? Was it just a case of immaturity, of poor judgment of risk versus reward? Was his lack of empathy at the root of his ruthless behaviour? What about the fact that his partners were just that for him, that they were not friends? Indeed, what about the fact that he didn't form actual friendships at all? How was it that his loyalties seemed to be selective? After all, he participated in seeing the Hortons, his erstwhile partners, thrown under the bus when they were unable to survive the predicament in which he placed them.

Instinctively, Teddy resisted my efforts to explore his reasons for acting as he did. Not that he was consciously aware of my presence, but he had trained himself so thoroughly to keep his thoughts to himself that he actually repressed his own motivations. He had learned to act swiftly, keeping his focus on achieving his goals, without consciously reasoning out all the intervening steps. The closest understanding I was able to achieve at that time was that he instinctively sought to achieve his overarching objective—which, in this case, had been to vault his partnership into a significantly more advanced sphere of business—while ignoring the possible and (in his view) temporary or insignificant side effects of his actions. A perhaps obtuse example of the ends justifying the means.

The kinds of restraints that are commonly rooted in a childhood where family connections, friendships, traditions, and long-established habits of behaviour that would usually limit the actions of a person so focused on a desired outcome simply didn't exist for Teddy. Hence, his actions were almost entirely driven by his perception of the desired outcome. Looking back on it now, I've come to understand that Teddy's relationship with the Simons, both father and son, quite apart from any specific incident, was hampered by their deep distrust of a man who carried with him no family traditions, no connection to ancestry, and no cultural models governing his behaviour. One discovery that offered me a bit of hope for him was that as far as I could determine, his actions in this particular case had nothing to do with personal profit at the expense of his partners. He had not sought personal glory or financial gain, but only what he perceived as a strategic advancement of the entire enterprise.

Teddy McCoy's motivations were far from being a simple, straightforward matter. There were times when his actions did not seem to follow any logical pattern, and it appeared to me that he sometimes did things simply to catch those people he regarded as opponents off balance; it was a variant on the pattern he had first established years earlier as a schoolboy, controlling the agenda of his Clan by thinking faster than his peers and always being a step ahead of them. There were no easy answers, no magic button that I could hope to push.

Of all the hosts I had adopted over my many centuries as a travelling spirit, I don't recall a single one who was as difficult to influence as Teddy McCoy. I believe that this was primarily due to the fact that he had never really lived within the give-and-take of a family unit, where each member of the family functions as a part of the whole, usually learning to accept limitations on their behaviour in the interest of family unity, and to maintain a measure of peace in the household. The influence of an actual parent, a person of authority who is not going to go away, one who is emotionally invested and has demonstrated a degree of empathy with the child, is bound to be greater than that of someone with whom the child has no real bond or sense of permanency in the relationship. And then, each successive stage in Teddy's early life tended to reinforce his sense of being on his own, a free agent, answerable to no one. He had become successful in disregarding those who sought to influence him and he saw no reason to change his behaviour.

But I also came to believe that his intransigence was an inborn aspect of his own personality, along with the sheer busy-ness of his hyperactive mind. He was constantly so engrossed in his own schemes, so intent on his own objectives, that his mind had no time or space left open for contemplating anyone else's ideas. In his own way, despite his constant interaction with others as his tempestuous career progressed, he led a lonely interior life.

It seemed to me that Teddy was having an intense long-term conversation with himself, to the exclusion of everyone else, including his resident soul. I don't offer any of this as an excuse for my failure to make effective contact and influence him. As a fully experienced spirit, I should have been well prepared to deal effectively with whatever host to which I found myself bound. I attribute a significant amount of the misfortune that was to befall

Teddy to my inability to steer him away from some of his mistakes. We were both complicit in Teddy McCoy's decisions, both the good and the bad.

****

Teddy's status within the company continued to evolve as their business grew over the next few years; his negotiating skills, his proficiency in the art of the deal greatly surpassed that of his more experienced partners, so that Teddy emerged as the public face of the consortium. He became highly creative in devising and introducing some unique feature in a proposal that would capture the attention of his potential customer and sway the decision in his company's favour, leaving his competitors shaking their heads in frustration. Contracts landed in that manner often proved to be more profitable than expected. He became the point man in dealing with the city; he learned how to grease the wheels with a modest favour to the right people at city hall.

By the age of twenty-six, Teddy had built up many useful contacts in both the business community and the municipal bureaucracy. Despite a less than polished demeanour and a somewhat murky reputation, he was on cordial terms with several influential politicians. Now a senior partner in SBT, he took the lead in contract negotiations. And he was becoming a very prosperous young man. He was invited to become a member of several golf and country clubs and regularly turned up at sod-turning and cornerstone ceremonies. He was also a man thoroughly detested by every trade unionist in and around Toronto.

The personality that I was intimately engaged with had been developing all this time in ways that I found, on the one hand, gratifying and at the same time deeply troubling. Teddy's instincts and actions were often contradictory: a take-no-prisoners mindset and a vicious way of doing business; he was thick skinned and brutal toward anyone who opposed him. He regarded rival contractors as outright enemies, and would do anything possible to take business away from them, discredit them, and disrupt their operations. With the help of his operatives, he planted rumours, accusing competitors of bid-rigging and shoddy workmanship.

And yet he was fiercely loyal to his supporters and highly protective of loyal members of his circle. He accumulated no real friends but he would defend his partners and employees almost without limit. Curiously, although Teddy disliked and distrusted all unions—believing them to be a cartel that enriched trouble-makers, layabouts, and charlatans, distorted the marketplace, and served the ordinary working man badly—he would go to great lengths to aid people he perceived as being mistreated by the rich and powerful. Whether I had any role in bringing out that side of Teddy, I cannot really say, but it was an aspect that convinced me that despite all his failings and his inauspicious beginnings, his was a personality with promise.

There was one episode in particular that illustrates what I mean. A powerful rival general contractor who was also a major real estate developer was aggressively buying up several blocks of property in a neighbourhood where Teddy had lived for several years. The area was composed mostly of aging row houses and semi-detached houses; there were a few small shops—a pizza place, a drycleaner, a bakery and deli, that sort of thing. And a tiny corner grocer that catered to the particular ethnic mix of the neighbourhood, primarily first-generation families of Southeast Asian, Caribbean, and Lebanese origins.

The grocer, a Vietnamese man in his late sixties, operated the store with his wife; they appeared to be just getting by and had no family to take over or help. But the store was very well established in the neighbourhood, and had become an informal drop-in spot for the locals to socialize and chat in a colourful mix of partially shared languages. The developer wanted to acquire that corner lot to complete his plans, and had been applying all kinds of pressure to force the grocer to sell; not by offering a high price but by telling him that all the houses nearby, where his customers lived, would soon be torn down; he should get out now because he would soon have no business.

But the aging couple knew only that neighbourhood, understood its wants and needs, and had invested a lifetime establishing rapport and loyalty; the business was not portable. Selling out would mean losing almost everything, including their own home above the store. It was their life. Teddy had found out what the developer was up to, what his game plan was, which particular blocks of land were critical to the success of his venture, which owners were open to being persuaded not to sell. He went to extreme lengths to thwart the development.

To keep residents in the neighbourhood even if the cash from the sale of their homes would be attractive to them, he began buying up aging houses that were strategically located, and thereby interfered with the development scheme. He fixed them up a bit and leased them—often back to the same owner-occupants he had bought them from. He brought his own company's crew in to renovate and upgrade the grocery at no cost to the owners. He walked all through the neighbourhood, accompanied by helpers who spoke the various languages common to the district, telling residents what was going on, urging them not to sell out, and encouraging them to continue supporting the corner store.

In the face of Teddy's campaign, the developer found it impossible to assemble the several blocks of land he needed; and it proved difficult to re-sell the houses he had already purchased. Several of them had fallen into such a serious state of disrepair that he was unable to lease them. The city would not issue permits to demolish them without also taking out a building permit to replace them. Because of the holdouts, he had acquired no single piece of land large enough for a high-rise building. He was likely going to lose money on every property he had acquired.

In the end, he was obliged to sell everything for whatever he could get, and the whole affair came close to forcing him into insolvency. Needless to say, he blamed Teddy McCoy's meddling for the failure of his scheme, and swore to even the score someday. Teddy derived an intense level of satisfaction from it all, even though it had cost him a significant amount of money to pull it off, money that he had fought long and ruthlessly to gain in a fiercely competitive business.

Although no one could deny that this venture of Teddy's into a form of social engineering was undertaken for an honourable cause, it hints at a troubling aspect of Teddy's belief system: that the end justifies the means. Over the years, he demonstrated many times a total disregard for the normal rules of engagement in his business dealings. Whatever Teddy set out to do, he was resolved to succeed in it, regardless of collateral damage along the way. That disregard for anything or anyone he saw as obstacles would lead Teddy into some very dark waters, and his motives were not always entirely honourable.

I had begun my assignment with Teddy handicapped by my recent experiences. I had participated in the uninspiring careers of several people one would not necessarily classify as overall failures but certainly no cause for celebration on my part. I needed to improve my game significantly, but so far Teddy wasn't developing into the most promising of candidates.

A man's life journey accompanied by the resident soul has to be a partnership for them to make a creditable job of it. If, on the day of his funeral, all that can be offered are a few mumbled excuses, not only is it too late for him to put things right; it's also too damn late for that unfortunate soul to improve its standing. You just have to move on to the next host and do the best you can under the circumstances. However, I wasn't entirely without resources. Despite my recent poor performance, I had over the course of my career acquired a lot of useful experience that I could bring to bear, notably tactics to capture the host's attention; and the ability to season my message to just the right flavour to appeal to my host's mindset.

Teddy had trained himself to ignore most of what his fellow humans attempted to tell him, so there was no chance he would listen to a completely inaudible voice seeking to reach him from some hidden recess within his mind. I understood that my only point of entry would be by way of invading his dreams, and even that was a long and tortuous road, a landscape cluttered with half-formed blobs of wishful thinking, juvenile fantasies, bizarre catastrophes, and violent confrontations with enemies both real and imagined. The noise level in the realm of Teddy's unconscious was deafening.

The other lesson I had long ago learned, that of carefully tailoring my message, held some small promise of success. In attempting to influence Teddy's unconscious tendencies—as a route toward eventually modifying his decisions, methods, and actions—I understood that urging him to do the right thing was certain to be a completely ineffective approach. Such a premise wasn't in his nature and if old Jung had it right, it would run contrary to the influence of the *collective unconscious* that Teddy had inherited from his forebears.

Furthermore, Teddy's early life experiences had taught him that it was best to seize the main chance. No, my pitch to Teddy had to be presented in terms such as "use your brain," "think longer term," or "consider all the alternatives and possible consequences." I won't pretend that any of this got through to him at first, but over time I think that I was influential in Teddy maturing into a somewhat more cautious man who took bold moves when conditions were right but had learned how to suppress the impulsive tendencies of his youth. That is not boasting; I recognize only too well that none of that went very far toward making Teddy an honourable human being.

Hustle

HAVING HUSTLED FOR EVERY CENT he ever owned, made his own way in an unforgiving world, and, never having had to thank anyone for his success, it's hardly surprising that Teddy McCoy felt entitled to more or less do as he pleased, as long as he stayed within the letter (if not necessarily the spirit) of the law. That applied to all aspects of his life, whether it be with the world of business, politics, or his personal relations with women.

Men like Teddy naturally attract certain kinds of associates, men who look to benefit by cruising along in the breeze created by a swift, successful operator. He also tended to attract certain kinds of women, the sort who smell easy money, good times, and a bit of excitement. From my position of intimate knowledge of Teddy's emotional state, I can declare that not one of these hopefuls continued to occupy any portion of his interest the moment he had his pants back on or she was out the door.

The parade of candidates for Teddy's attentions had begun early, when the Clan first established itself in its sector of the city; and the parade never really ended. As Teddy's career progressed and his income level improved, impressionable teenagers were in due course replaced by a series of dancers, strippers, and would-be starlets. Each of them in turn was eventually brought face to face with the reality of their replaceable status and lack of uniqueness—when Teddy dumped them.

Then there was Cassie. Conducting himself as he did, it was inevitable that Teddy would encounter a woman the likes of Cassie, one who understood this game as well as he did. She possessed the skills, connections and savvy to establish a claim on him in ways that he couldn't walk away from with a simple "See ya later, babe!" Cassie had learned to listen attentively to what was being said in private between city bureaucrats and others, when she was supposed to have simply been hanging around as arm candy, serving as a bit of decoration in Teddy's retinue. When Teddy's interest in Cassie waned, he discovered that it was going to take a lot more than a pair of fake diamond earrings and a farewell card to change her status to some word beginning with *ex-*.

The day after Teddy had given Cassie what he thought was the usual brush-off, he received a very tense phone call from a city councillor, insisting on having a private meeting to discuss certain allegations that were apparently about to be brought to the attention of the local media. Teddy, not having previously faced anything of this nature, endeavoured to reassure the councillor that he had nothing to be concerned about. The councillor was not in the least satisfied with Teddy's response; he insisted on a personal meeting, during which he displayed a photocopy of a document that both of them had previously believed to exist only in a locked filing cabinet that no one else knew about, and of which there had never been another copy.

With a great deal of consternation (all of which I was intimately exposed to) Teddy took the measures necessary to satisfy Cassie's requirements to make the matter go away. In doing so, Teddy displayed all the caution and prudence in crisis management that he had learned along the way. Having clearly understood the vulnerability of his position, he brought all of his best negotiating and deal-making abilities into play. The agreement he reached with Cassie was crafted in such a way as to leave Cassie completely satisfied to walk away feeling like a winner, while also leaving her unable to reopen the matter at a later date without imperilling her livelihood, health, and personal reputation.

The experience left Teddy with a lesson in self-preservation that remained firmly established for the rest of his life. It also hardened his approach to casual relationships, causing him to be far more selective in his choice of personal companions. After that experience, he was never again seen to have any of his female companions present where business discussions took place. He also began to think in terms of a relationship with a woman as part of some kind of strategic arrangement, rather than just decoration and personal amusement.

That was when Teddy McCoy first began to take an interest in the daughters of people he did business with. He learned to look beyond the financial considerations in business relationships and look into the social standing and family connections of the people he encountered. Teddy, the eternal outsider, was beginning to search for a route into the mainstream. His life experiences to that point fell far short of preparing him for such an endeavour; but then, Teddy was a fast learner and had no shortage of moxie.

The bleakness of Teddy's emotional life, discoloured as it was by his absence of any personal family connections, and further smudged through a lengthy series of frivolous affairs and betrayals, became an increasing concern to me. Although there was not a complete absence of humanity in this man, his outlook on life, his valuation of people, was distorted. Though successful in his business career, Teddy was by no means a happy man. Having to continually watch his back in his business life had also translated into instinctively looking over his shoulder socially, distrusting women, and focusing on ensuring his own best interests. His emerging interest in the idea of a strategic relationship with a woman as an adjunct to his career, rather than as a life partner, was not necessarily an encouraging development.

****

It was unavoidable that Teddy would accumulate enemies, and not just among the trade unions. As his business grew, he found it increasingly difficult to secure major contracts without impacting the interests of business rivals. There were also elements at city hall as well as property developers who deeply distrusted Teddy and his associates and were convinced that he was engaged in unsavoury practices. In this they were correct, but Teddy had learned to cover his tracks very well, and those officials he dealt with also had powerful reasons for keeping the nature of their involvement from being known.

Apart from the unions, Teddy's number one enemy was a property development group named Silver Associates. Howard Silver, the CEO and majority owner of that company, had long since made his peace with the building trade unions, and he bitterly resented Teddy's ability to engage lower-cost non-union crews. He was certain that illicit payments were being made in certain quarters to land contracts, but he was unable to obtain a shred of evidence to support any such allegation.

Howard Silver stood for everything that Teddy McCoy and his colleagues were not: widely respected, conventional in his business dealings, tolerant of the building trade unions. A man who *belonged*. Howard Silver's presence was a constant reminder of what Teddy McCoy was lacking. Teddy understood that in order to compete with a man like Howard Silver, it would always be necessary for him to run faster, play the game harder, work the angles, and cut corners. The animosity between McCoy's partners and Silver's people grew more vehement every time their paths crossed; which was often, since they were frequently bidding against each other. The hatred between McCoy and Silver became personal, each determined to undermine the other in any way possible.

Howard Silver could not figure out how Teddy and his partners managed to undercut him on one contract after another. He was determined to discover what was going on and put a stop to it. Silver made it his business to find an agent with deep knowledge of the local contracting environment as well as union activities, hoping thereby to not only get some dirt on Teddy and his partners but also to discover why the unions were so lacking in success in dealing with Teddy. Silver was elated when he discovered the existence of a private investigator with exactly the qualifications he sought, an agency that no one seemed to know anything about. He met with them secretly and laid out his requirements. They agreed to take on the job for him. The fees they quoted were so modest that he ought to have realized something was fishy, but he was so eager to finally catch up with Teddy that he engaged them immediately.

What Silver couldn't know was that Teddy had secretly organized a small group of his former Clan members into a private detective agency, totally owned by Teddy McCoy; this numbered company's ownership was not public knowledge. The agency's sole purpose was to keep tabs on union activity while also discovering who was planning to bid on upcoming projects and find out who the real decision makers were in the awarding of contracts. And along the way, the agency was to figure out who could be bought and who might be vulnerable to a bit of arm-twisting or threat of exposure of their past misdeeds.

When Silver had gone looking for an agent, Teddy's fellows got wind of it immediately and made sure that Silver would stumble onto them, unaware of the agency's ownership. The outcome was entirely predictable, and catastrophic for Silver Associates.

The detective agency fed Silver enough real information to keep him interested, but nothing that he could use against his enemy. At that time, the city was preparing to let a very large contract that both Teddy's firm and Silver were determined to land. The detectives, ostensibly after some serious digging for inside information, informed Silver that mischief was afoot. The real value of the contract had been artificially inflated by city officials in collusion with Teddy's firm in order to drive bid prices higher. Teddy would be sure to land the contract by quoting a figure 10 percent below this grossly inflated value, and a small group of city officials would be paid a substantial kickback.

To secure the contract, Silver would need to bid even lower. Based on the misleading information in the published tender, such a low bid would appear to put Teddy's company in a loss position before the project ever got under way. No other company bidding on what had been publicly presented would be foolhardy enough to enter such a bid, so unless Silver took action to thwart him, Teddy's company was sure to win.

Howard Silver pounced; he submitted an even bid lower than Teddy's, at what he saw as a break-even amount. He wouldn't make much on the contract, but hoped to pick up a bit of money on the usual contract extras. The real triumph would be in depriving both Teddy and the corrupt officials of their bounty. Silver Associates was duly awarded the contract, and the city was delighted at the low price.

Within a few weeks, once Silver's project team gained a better understanding of the detailed requirements, the real truth emerged. The value had not been inflated at all; in fact, faced with Silver's low bid, Teddy's company had withdrawn its own offer, to make sure that Silver would not be able to back down. Having no other viable alternative, the city would be sure to hold Silver to his proposal.

When Silver furiously confronted the detective agency with the errors in the information they had provided, they pointed out that in taking on his assignment, their offer of services made no specific guarantee of accuracy, just a pledge to provide the best intelligence available to them. Obviously, some unnamed individuals at city hall or elsewhere had provided inaccurate data. Their agreement with Silver also explicitly stated that their sources of information could never be divulged. It was, after all, essential for such an agency to be able to protect its informants.

It was now abundantly clear to Silver that he was going to lose a lot of money on this contract; he had no recourse but to suffer through it and hope to recover at least part of his losses elsewhere. Meanwhile, the contract itself was so big that he had no resources to take on anything else of major size until that work was finished.

Teddy was far from being finished with this gambit. What Silver also didn't know was that Teddy had, for several years, been keeping union organizers away from his business by the simple means of bribing several of the key organizers to steer clear of his contracts. While Teddy openly denounced the unions in public and personally detested them, he had no qualms about buying them off. The fact that some of the union officials were willing to accept payoffs, to the serious disadvantage of the workers for whom they pretended to advocate, simply proved to Teddy how corrupt they were.

I had found myself embedded with a man who had sincerely convinced himself that this whole insidious arrangement was not only legitimate, but even honourable. Penetrating beyond Teddy's aggressive, self-justifying ego had proven almost impossible. Human nature is such that the higher the financial advantage at stake, the easier it becomes for people to talk themselves into corrupt practices.

Early in the term of Silver's unfortunate contract, several of the trades engaged on it were coming to the end of their collective agreements. Silver, having made peace with the unions and having loudly condemned Teddy's union-bashing, had not encountered labour difficulties for many years; he expected to get new agreements signed quickly with no hassle. In this, he was sadly mistaken. The locals in every trade began placing extraordinary new demands on the table; wages were at risk of spiralling out of control. I knew (while no one else ever did) that Teddy had encouraged the union leaders to present excessive demands, while assuring them that Silver was in a jam and would have to capitulate. Within a month, the entire project was strike-bound.

Silver Associates was protected against penalties being levied by the city for non-performance because of a force majeure clause that included labour stoppages. But while work was stopped, progress payments also stopped. Silver had no income, and he soon had a cash flow shortfall of major proportions. Then things got even worse: the force majeure provision had a time limit on it, to protect the city in the event of a contractor stubbornly failing to negotiate a collective agreement in good faith. If work did not get under way within 90 days, penalties would be applied. Silver would have to agree to the union demands. By this time, he was truly desperate to find a way out of his dilemma.

That was when Teddy played his final card. Knowing that the city was extremely eager to get the work under way, he secretly reached an agreement with city officials to look away if Silver were to bring in strike-breakers; he offered to provide Silver with non-union workforces to complete his contract. Facing certain bankruptcy, Silver had no option but to accept the offer. The contract was completed in that manner, but Silver's reputation was in ruins and the unions were so angry with him for strike-breaking that he found it almost impossible to operate thereafter. Silver Associates declared bankruptcy a year later and Howard Silver retired, a broken man.

He had, of course, come to understand how this had happened and who was responsible for it, but it was too late. There was nothing he could do about it other than write angry letters to the newspapers and publicly demand an investigation into Teddy McCoy's practices—none of which happened; Teddy's contacts in the right quarters made sure of that.

In Teddy's defense, it might be pointed out that Howard Silver was a big boy, an experienced, well-established businessman twenty-two years senior to a relative upstart like Teddy McCoy. You may say that Silver should have been able to look after his own interests; that he had deliberately set out to damage Teddy's business and got caught in his own trap. Business is business, and there's no place in that arena for weakness or incompetence.

But I'm afraid that won't wash. The plain truth is that Howard Silver's downfall was deliberately engineered by Teddy McCoy for his own selfish reasons, and he was gleeful in doing so. Nor can I claim to have succeeded in diverting his attention or influencing him toward restraint in any way. It was not for lack of trying, but in my weakened state, my performance thus far had been inept. Nor was this a unique event; Teddy didn't treat other opponents in business fairly at all times, either. Teddy McCoy was a project that was going to demand every bit of my experience and skill; my prospects for success were bleak.

In each of my engagements, I'm continually faced with this infernal, inescapable obligation: I have a life on my hands here. I cannot drop this mortal that has been placed in my care, never mind my limited ability to influence its actions. There is no forgiveness for me, no excuses available.

You mortals are accustomed to arguing your fate, negotiating for a lighter sentence. You've even created special classes of humans to intercede on your behalf, called lawyers and priests. Those of you of a religious mindset even presume to argue your case with God! "If you let me off this time, I promise to be a better person from now on!" No such escape route is possible for me because I'm up against the sternest, most implacable judge of all: my own knowledge of the facts. Should I fail in my mission, I must carry that burden of failure with me forever; there is no means of erasing it from my record.

So you see, those suffering spirits that can obtain no relief, those tortured souls that you are told about in your ghost stories—they really do exist. They are spirits that have fallen down on their job. The resulting trauma experienced by their mortal host comes to an end at their death. No such relief is possible for the soul that has let them down.

A Shock

ACCOMPANYING TEDDY AS HE PURSUED his aggressive career, as he became increasingly adept at playing a brutal game, I could foresee this being an engagement that would add one more to my list of failures. Even if I had found ways to engage more fully with his persona, it was going to be a difficult assignment, keeping Teddy from spinning entirely out of control. His life experiences had taught him neither humility nor a lot of compassion.

The human animal is burdened with an acquisitive, self-serving instinct. The man who finds himself on a path toward ascendancy becomes addicted to his own success, the thrill of victory. Conversely, the man who finds himself on the losing end of battles against his peers often becomes vicious, developing a "me against the world" mentality, leading him to resort to the vilest sort of tactics; and he believes himself justified in doing so.

With his driven personality, Teddy was at risk of either of those possible outcomes. A soul finding itself unable to modify its host's belief system and state of mind can find itself spun along on a career that can only end in tragedy for those people who fall under the host's power; and in the end, the host falls victim to his own misdeeds. Hence, the long, sad history of despotism and mayhem for which mankind is known.

The companions of Teddy's youth (and the cohort by which he was now surrounded) had reinforced his self-image as the street-wise, two-fisted outsider, the tough kid who had made good. The women he had associated with had either nourished his ego or betrayed his trust. He was finding his way into a society where people pretended to value honesty, tolerance, and forbearance while, in reality, they were taking every opportunity to look after number one.

Teddy's inborn mistrust of people's motives was validated by the hypocrisy that he observed. He had invested a lot of effort into learning how to play the game. Taking part in opening ceremonies, fundraisers, galas, and the like was helping Teddy to polish his public face; he was rapidly learning the jargon of feigned sincerity and understanding the value of the photo-op. Exposure to politicians was not improving his general opinion of humanity.

Early in 1993, as lead contractor on the building of a new wing onto an aging hospital, Teddy was front and centre at a ribbon-cutting ceremony, attended by the usual assemblage of politicos, do-gooders, and social climbers. Some aging millionaire, wishing to appear to atone for his former misdeeds, had sponsored an impressive bronze sculpture to grace the new entrance to the building.

It was impossible to say what benefit the placement of this artwork offered to a critically ill patient or a parent with a desperately sick child as they arrived at the hospital. But no one was about to spoil the day by suggesting that the gesture was misplaced. Perhaps it would help to raise the spirits of some of the overstressed and underpaid nurses as they staggered home from another double shift. Teddy didn't concern himself with such speculations. He did as he had learned to do: just go along with it all, smile for the cameras, and look businesslike, as the occasion demanded.

He found himself being posed for a publicity photo next to the sculptor who had created this piece of public art. She turned out to be a slightly built woman in her late twenties, who Teddy would hardly have expected to be found building the mould for a piece of bronze that must have weighed at least 2 tons. Her reserved, appraising gaze struck him as less than reassuring. Cool grey eyes that seemed not to be looking at Teddy, the man, his face, his figure, his persona as entrepreneur, successful contractor. Instead, he had an uncomfortable feeling that she was peering into the essence of Teddy, the human being, the boy who had been shuffled around by a largely hostile world, the fellow who had often been made to feel unwelcome or unworthy.

This aggravating woman would not be one that Teddy wished to have dealings with. He could not have told anyone why it should be the case, but he was certain that his personal accomplishments, his prosperity, and his physical attributes would count for nothing in forming this woman's opinion of him. Here was a kind of woman that Teddy had never before encountered closely, and one that he had no inkling of how to deal with. He picked up on her name as Ellen Bruce, surely a Scottish name; and he detected a very slight pattern to her speech that suggested at least an exposure to the land of haggis and tartans. Apart from that, he had never heard of the dame, and expected that after this phony ceremony was over, he would never encounter her again; and a good thing, too.

On first meeting her, most people would describe Ellen Bruce as impressive and yet unremarkable; perhaps handsome rather than beautiful: trim and very fit-looking, below average height, a face that would be thought of as strong, placid, self-confident, topped with a short, simple, no-nonsense hairdo that would likely require very little maintenance. A light of penetrating intelligence shone in those quiet grey eyes. The women Teddy usually associated with tended to come in fancier packages, and their agendas were a lot easier to read.

Teddy's instinctive aversion to her was further reinforced by the object that stood at the centre of everyone's attention that day: a burnished piece of yellow-brown metal depicting, in a somewhat subdued manner, what appeared to be a woman in nurse's attire leaning over a frightened-looking child. This was almost but not quite representational art; the two figures were clearly human, but they were not presented as individuals, living persons who would have names, addresses, SIN numbers, allergies, prejudices; rather, they were characters caught at an instant in a generic human drama, archetypes of a relationship, a vignette captured from the ongoing story of the patient, the comforter, and the anticipation of what was about to happen next.

Rather than diverting Teddy's attention away from its somewhat annoying creator, the sculpture itself curiously added to his unease with its maker. He found himself reacting strongly to the work; it disturbed him and he could not have pinpointed any reason for that. It was, after all, just a big chunk of cast metal, the result of a process that had begun with a mound of wet clay, evolved in a foundry, and finished up with a good deal of painstaking work on its graceful surfaces. He couldn't see anything the least bit remarkable about it, nor did it have any bearing whatsoever on Teddy's life, his prospects, his welfare, or his interests. He resolved that as soon as this bit of nonsense and the boring speeches that went along with it were over, he would not have anything more to do with the woman or her artistic endeavours.

Teddy, being Teddy, had other reasons for attending the event apart from a boring and somewhat pointless photo-op; it was his chance to meet with a senior city manager to explore upcoming projects, begin preparing a path toward an advantageous position when the bidding opened. With that in mind, and already looking forward to the useful part of his day, he was taken aback to discover that the fellow he was so eager to engage was a personal friend of the sculptor, and had probably played some role in her having landed the commission in the first place. Nevertheless, not wishing to miss out on a business opportunity, Teddy invited the man to lunch anyway, and when he accepted and in turn asked Ellen Bruce to join them, there was no way for Teddy to back out.

Teddy's misgivings about that lunch proved to have been well founded. The conversation kept drifting onto what Ellen Bruce had been doing and where she stood in the exotic world of art, an environment entirely beyond Teddy's competence. He was unable to steer the encounter in a direction that would offer him an opening that might lead to the business at hand, let alone any future business advantage. The entire day was turning into not just a colossal waste of time, but a thoroughly frustrating and unsettling experience.

Ellen, on the other hand, was entirely in her element, clearly in control of the discussion and confident of her position of strength relative to the two men. It irked Teddy to recognize this fact, given that she was, in theory, dependent on this man and the decisions of his associates for her livelihood. And she could not possibly have any power over Teddy, a man who was accustomed to handling complex business relationships, and who understood the role of women in his world and made sure they always got the message.

Finding himself increasingly marginalized in the ongoing conversation, his attention began to wander, and he was unable to keep from fidgeting. Each time a remark or a question was directed to him, he was unprepared to respond in any way that would help his cause. The topics of discussion had no relevance to his purpose in being there, and his awkward attempts to take part in what was being discussed sounded as if he had stumbled into the wrong party. He was considering a graceful departure from the scene when he was jolted back into the middle of it all by this aggravating woman. She suddenly addressed Teddy directly. "Mr. McCoy, do I make you feel uncomfortable? You seem a bit distracted."

It was a rare event for Teddy to find himself lost for words. He could only respond, with hesitation, "I don't get what you mean.

I'm just sitting here listening to you two talk about… I don't know… stuff."

She was obviously amused at his discomfort, not at all hostile but singularly unimpressed by Teddy McCoy. "I'm not trying to put you down. I'm quite sure you don't allow anyone to do that to you. You're an important man in this town. Everyone knows that. I'm just a struggling artist."

Teddy struggled to keep his composure. "I do alright and I guess you do, too, in your own way. But let's face it, we probably come from different planets."

"Perhaps if we had met under different circumstances, you and I might actually find some tiny area of common interest. After all, in our own ways, we both build things. Isn't that so? I hope you won't go away thinking too badly of me. I can't afford to make enemies; I understand that's something that you never trouble yourself about."

She was really getting under Teddy's skin, and he couldn't for the life of him understand why she wished to do so; or why he should care. With effort, he kept himself from lashing out at her and simply mumbled something about having overstayed his welcome and needing to attend to business. After some further awkward exchanges, they bid abrupt farewells and Teddy departed, leaving the two of them to their coffee and fussy little desserts. Simultaneously annoyed and relieved, Teddy expected never to meet the woman again. He made up his mind to just forget about her.

But a couple of days later, a bottle of wine was delivered to his office, accompanied by a note from Ellen Bruce.

> *I'm afraid I was very rude to you the other day and I want to apologize. I don't ordinarily treat strangers (or anyone else) that way. The truth is that men like you often tend to intimidate me and I guess I was*

overcompensating. I hope you will forgive me. I see your work all over the city; you've seen only one bit of mine. If you should care to drop by my studio one day, perhaps I could convince you that I'm not really a bitch after all, and that what I do is worthwhile. I'm here almost every day, since I live in a loft above my workshop. I promise not to attack you and I'll not subject you to silly little pastries, which I noticed you dislike. I've sent wine because I don't know your taste. Perhaps Scotch would have been more to your liking.

It took Teddy several days to make up his mind how to react to that overture. His first instinct was to throw that damn bottle in the trash along with her note. Any involvement with such a woman, an artist, could not possibly do him any good and she was sure to be a distraction at best and, more likely, a bundle of trouble; the fact that some of the city officials were her friends could complicate matters.

Above all, there was something about her personality that disturbed him. And yet the very fact that she bothered him suggested that by ignoring her, he was somehow running away; and that idea infuriated him. He also understood that if he did see her again in his current state of mind, they were likely to get into a row; that would serve no purpose whatever, and would possibly make enemies for him among important people who happened to be her friends. Best to just forget about the whole thing. Or even better, send back a polite note, thanking her for her gift and giving her the brush-off. After all, that was something Teddy certainly knew how to do.

You might expect that, as a widely experienced and reasonably competent spiritual sidekick, I would have stepped in here and offered my host a bit of sage advice, or at least a measure of self-confidence, the ability to make a rational decision. You would be disappointed. I did no such thing, being as irresolute in my spirit as was Teddy in his mind. I suppose if the man I was embedded with had been a fellow whose life ran in straighter lines, who operated from a position of honorability in his dealings with women, it would have been easier for me to nudge my host in the right direction. But if my host had been that sort of man to begin with, perhaps the uncertainty would never have arisen.

Am I making excuses here? Maybe I am. Anyway, the truth of the matter is that I provided no help, leaving Teddy to figure it out for himself.

Three days passed with the bottle still resting on a shelf behind his desk, tantalizing him. His note back to Ellen had been written and destroyed several times. How was it possible for that dame to get to him that way? When he woke up each morning, her damnable note was the first thing that popped into his mind. Teddy had always been completely unable to tolerate indecision in himself; if he detected it in others, he recognized it as a point of weakness, and took full advantage of it by decisive action. He was determined to resolve the matter one way or another.

So on the fourth day following receipt of the note, he phoned Ellen, and when she answered, he refused to allow her to talk, simply informing her that he was heading over to her studio immediately and hanging up. He had convinced himself that taking this action as abruptly as he did would settle the matter in his own mind and put Ellen on notice that he was not a man to be played with. He foresaw the possibility of an unpleasant confrontation, but there was no turning back. By the time he arrived, he was sure he had made a horrible blunder, and contemplated ways that he might be able to exit quietly.

He found Ellen calmly at work. She didn't comment on his rude phone call or anything else, just invited him to look around at what she had been working on while she washed some of the stone dust, clay, and paint off her hands. She pointed him to a selection of liquor and wines on a small sideboard and invited him to serve himself. "There's beer and such in that fridge, if you prefer."

Teddy, despite having no knowledge of sculpture or art in general, found some of her work to be of great interest. The antagonism he had expected never materialized, although there remained something about Ellen that made him feel unsure of himself. He could not resist the urge to try to discover what this woman was all about; and, more to the point, why she had invited him there at all. With Teddy, the most direct approach was the one he would be most likely to take. He put the question to her simply. "I still don't understand why you sent that note. You and I live in two different worlds. Why bother with a roughneck like me?"

"I'm not at all sure I know the answer to that, except that I've never encountered anyone quite like you, at least not on a personal basis. I suppose you arouse my curiosity. I'm a curious person. You see, I've studied a lot of very different things besides sculpture.

"My dad was a merchant sailor, captain of several large ocean freighters. My mother died when I was only six years old and I travelled all over the world with my dad. I went to school for a couple of years in India, then the Philippines, never actually finished high school. I got interested in art, hung around various kinds of workshops and foundries in Scotland where I lived for a few years. I got to know something about the science of materials in Germany. Along the way, I've taken a great interest in people, how they think, what motivates them. I'm a terrible snoop (not a gossip, mind you); I've gotten to know quite a lot about you. I know how you came to be the man you are and you intrigue me. I guess it's as simple as that.

"By the way, I'm not at all sure that I like you. You must realize that you rub a lot of people the wrong way; and I doubt if that bothers you too much, so I don't think I have to worry a great deal about hurting your feelings. That sort of makes it easier for me to deal with you. After having to put up with the comments I get from art critics and other self-appointed experts, I've become pretty thick skinned myself. You're not likely to offend me with your opinions, so I don't see why we can't get along."

Over the next hour, these two entirely mismatched people discovered that they could throw frank comments back and forth, ask intrusive questions, generally fail to agree on any topic at all, and yet find the encounter surprisingly invigorating. They had made serious inroads into a bottle of Scotch and resolved to meet again to continue the discussion.

Although Teddy had found the afternoon a fascinating experience, he remained ill at ease, unsure about why he was interested in this unusual woman. She bore no resemblance to any of the women he had pursued before, and he didn't actually find her visually alluring. She contradicted all of his views on what a woman should be, how she should act, or what benefit she would be likely to provide for him. She seemed to lack everything that he had ever found attractive in a woman. But pursue her, he did.

And what of *her* resident soul? Surely, you would expect that I knew all about that. Sadly, that was not the case. You see, it's like this: souls lead what you would likely see as a lonely existence, in a realm where time and space have no meaning. You might have assumed that we communicate with each other, understand what other souls are about, that perhaps we can assist each other in dealing with problematic hosts. But that is not the way it works; making contact is difficult.

There have been times in my past when I've been able to connect with another soul, one that resided with someone close to my host. But that's never easy to accomplish and it may turn out to be very painful, rather than gratifying; or even useful. Whatever I had been able to learn about Ellen, her life, her personality, her passions I had to gain by observation of her behaviour and, indirectly, through what Teddy himself came to discover.

Although they seemed such an unlikely match, they had more in common than would have been immediately obvious. To begin with, both were lacking in formal education. Banging around the world as she had in her youth, where almost everyone's livelihood was connected with the making of things at the most basic level, Ellen was a creature of the workshop floor, not the formality of the lecture hall. Her work was the product of instinct rather than formal artistic training.

She had never studied sculpture under any teacher or mentor; she had created figures in clay since childhood, had taught herself to carve in wood and stone. She had learned metalwork by hanging around tradesmen and labourers. She knew a great deal about the workings of a bronze foundry. She also knew how works of art came to be chosen and featured in public places and therefore, understood a lot about how politicians and wealthy patrons think and act. On the other hand, an aggressive entrepreneur like Teddy was entirely new to her.

She had taught herself a bit about the history of art while never taking either conventional ideas or the current trends in art very seriously. Her choices of subject matter, even when responding to a commission, were largely driven by her own inner beliefs. Her style was entirely her own. Like Teddy, she was an outsider in her chosen field.

It became clear to me that she was a passionate but very private person. Those traits had become reinforced by the reaction that her work garnered among the art world intelligentsia. Fellow artists and most critics sniffed at her work as reactionary and "pretty," that term apparently relegating her to amateur status, or worse. All of which she happily ignored. Municipalities and more than a few corporations appeared to appreciate her work, awarding her a number of generous commissions, a fact that incurred the intense displeasure of those who were assumed to be in the know. And their antagonism provided Ellen with a good deal of personal satisfaction, along with the pleasure of cashing the sponsors' cheques.

Ellen's works were representational, not of the physical form of her subjects, but rather of their mental or emotional state. Teddy reacted strongly to them. They unsettled him, but he could not understand why that should be so. On his first visit to Ellen's studio, he confronted a bronze sculpture depicting a homeless woman, dressed in rags, seemingly huddled against the cold; he experienced simultaneously both sympathy and revulsion. He at first pretended to ignore the piece, taking their discussions onto other topics, but Ellen was far too observant and too willful to allow him to escape her scrutiny.

She challenged him to make known his opinion of the work and then defend his point of view, thereby confirming her expectation that while he was lacking in knowledge of the topic at hand, he could react quickly and think on his feet. The subliminal messages that often emerge from a work of art were not lost on Teddy, whether he possessed the vocabulary to express them or not. By some process I don't begin to understand, that dark bronze image of a homeless woman must have become permanently etched into Teddy's subconscious mind, seemingly forgotten, only to resurface many years later in a way that no one could have foreseen.

I didn't realize it at that moment, but I grew to understand that even though Teddy's manner could be irritating, Ellen had sensed in Teddy the presence of a kindred personality. She found his quick mind and his blunt, no-nonsense way of stating his opinions (and challenging hers) both stimulating and refreshing, compared with the nuanced but often phony discussions she encountered with others in the artistic community. Rather than being repelled by his crude exterior and apparent truculence, she was attracted. Smooth-talking charmers, on the other hand, were the kind of men that she distrusted and could not abide.

****

Over that summer, a routine developed; they would meet for dinner several times a week at one or another local restaurant; not upscale places, but usually spots where the food was uncomplicated and it was quiet enough to hold a conversation. Teddy was discovering a vast array of topics about which he had been entirely unaware. Their discussion would continue at Ellen's studio, often late into the night. He never kissed her, made no physical advances, and told himself that she meant nothing to him; she was just an intellectual challenge, a mental adversary against whom he could sharpen his wits and with whom almost any topic was open for debate. They argued constantly, not belligerently, but with determination.

A soul is so intimately engaged in attempting to understand and influence its host that it's usually difficult to gain a clear insight into the personality of each of the other mortals surrounding its host. We're not terribly adept at judging people by their physical characteristics (which perhaps is just as well). We focus on behaviour and whatever signals we can pick up indicating what manner of soul inhabits each of them. And that is almost always difficult. If someone seems to have little importance to the life of our host, we more or less ignore them. So it took me quite some time to develop as clear an insight into the persona of Ellen Bruce as I would have liked.

I eventually saw that she was very much a product of her vagabond upbringing, skipping around all over the world, tagging after her seagoing father. She had often been much more on her own than most girls would have been at the same age. She developed into a self-aware and self-actualizing free spirit, comfortable with finding herself an outsider.

She related well to the blunt, plainspoken workmen that she encountered in factories and foundries; she was usually distrustful of anyone who projected an aura of sophistication. She had no patience with fussy, image-conscious people; hence, her avoidance of hairdressers and her almost boyish choice of coiffure. She preferred pub food over fancy fare, beer over fine wine, and jeans over dresses. Like Teddy, she resented authority figures unless they were able to convince her of their soundness of judgment and impartiality of mind.

The sculptures Ellen created were all, in one way or another, expressions of her own worldview. Much could be gleaned about her personality, beliefs, and mindset through a careful examination of her works. Once she had made up her mind about a person or an issue, Ellen could be just as implacable as Teddy.

I know that Teddy became aware of the existence of these traits and the strength of character that prevailed in Ellen Bruce; but I doubt if he had an understanding of her code of honour and what a stark danger all of those attributes presented to any man who lived the way he did.

Over centuries of close association with strong-minded men, I've noticed that the points of inflection in their careers are often marked by the arrival and influence of women such as Ellen Bruce. She gradually became the centre of his attention during every waking hour when he was not deeply engaged in the business of making Teddy McCoy wealthy. Before long, she had begun to invade his thoughts even while he was in the midst of business pursuits.

And then, the night that Ellen appeared full force in his dreams shocked Teddy to the core. What on earth was happening to him? He didn't mention it to Ellen, hoping that it was just an aberration. But a day later, Ellen phoned to tell him that she had accepted a commission for a set of sculptures to be placed at the approaches to a new bridge in Vancouver and she would be out west for the next two weeks getting the layout, scale, and sightlines sorted out. To Teddy's dismay, while she was away, he found himself lost in daydreams, unable to sleep, uninterested in anything, be it food, companions, or business. Each night when sleep finally came, Ellen haunted his every dream.

For the first time in his life, Teddy McCoy was utterly terrified and helpless. He finally understood with a shock that he had fallen in love with Ellen Bruce. What was worse, she was phoning him every night, admitting that she missed him terribly, and that she was constantly dreaming about him. These two were of no use to each other. Their lifestyles were incompatible; they constantly disagreed on everything imaginable. Their fundamental belief systems were at odds and they would be sure to find it impossible to live together.

But Ellen cut her Vancouver trip short, flew home, and fell into Teddy's panic-stricken arms. Before they had any idea what was happening to them, they found themselves in bed. To Teddy's further dismay, he discovered that despite being at odds on almost any other topic, they were gloriously compatible sexually.

Something had to be done about this, but what?

Teddy's life had always been hard edged, like an army cot, a wooden church pew, a walk against the wind on a rainy night; never comfortable, if you get my meaning. You can sleep on a hard cot; you can pray from a rigid bench; a rainy walk can take you where you need to go. But there's always something missing in such a life. What was missing in Teddy's life was what I can best describe as an *attachment*. What I mean by an attachment has nothing to do with a biological relationship; it doesn't require the presence of love in the usual sense—although love may come to play a part in it. An attachment is something that arises between the souls that have taken up residence with two humans during their lives.

Teddy's isolated existence was largely the fault of his disconnected upbringing. There was no place that Teddy would have thought of as *home*. He never had a real family, his "Clan" having had to fill his need for belonging. He was beholden to no one, had many associates but no friends. He had never even owned a dog.

But there's another side to Teddy's dilemma, and whatever is amiss in that quarter can be laid on my doorstep. If ever Teddy were to find what you may call a soulmate—well, I would have to be the primary conduit, the link to a kindred spirit. But I entered this arena in a somewhat damaged state. Poorly prepared souls don't perform well in enabling their hosts to form an attachment. In this situation, the delicate business of reaching out to another soul, I was the ugly girl at the party and I was not expecting many invitations to dance.

I had not been able to make any sort of contact with the soul that was accompanying Ellen on her life journey. I had little to offer that might help to open the doors; I was entirely shut out. Nor did I have reason to believe that an attachment between us stood any chance of success. So the relationship between Teddy and Ellen existed only on a biological and intellectual level; they were drawn to each other, but there was no common ground between their resident souls. Lovers who cannot become soulmates are often doomed from the outset. They cannot bear to be apart and yet they cannot function together. Their orbits cross, but they're spinning in opposite directions.

Teddy had no roadmap for the territory in which he had suddenly found himself; his emotional need for Ellen rendered him vulnerable to a degree he had never before experienced. And you may find this hard to understand, but I was sharing his terror. I knew that I was about to fail him utterly at this critical point in his life.

When they first met, hoping that with her entirely different personality and beliefs she would be a positive influence on Teddy, I had encouraged the relationship to the extent that I was able to do so. To achieve that, my breakthrough was by means of manipulating those dreams. I admit that it was I who had enhanced the presence of Ellen in Teddy's dreams, even though I had not been able to reach Ellen through her resident spirit. She fell in love with Teddy almost from the beginning, all by herself. It was only some time later that I saw I had made a terrible blunder. This love affair was headed for disaster and I admit that some of it was my fault.

Teddy did something he had never done before other than that time he set fire to the Allwoods' house: he ran away in sheer panic.

He had to get away from Ellen to sort himself out. Not only did her presence overwhelm his ability to think clearly and function rationally, but an alliance with her was unthinkable from a practical standpoint. He couldn't possibly consider marrying Ellen. He had long since made up his mind about what kind of wife he would need to find, the kind of alliance that would take him where he planned to go; and he was determined to make that happen.

He had to find a way to dump Ellen.

Hard. And fast.

Teddy was perceptive enough to understand that it was necessary to give Ellen cause to hate him, otherwise she would continue to cling to some troublesome hope of reconciliation; even worse, to blame herself for the break and seek ways to repair it. It was essential that Teddy accept the role as the "bad guy", the heartless, selfish S.O.B. who had betrayed her and thrown it all away. That prospect didn't particularly disturb him, since Teddy had behaved in a similar manner any number of times when it had suited him, and the acquisition of another bitter enemy didn't trouble him.

If only it had been that easy.

He began by going shopping. He acquired an outrageously expensive diamond bracelet and had it sent to Ellen, accompanied by a carefully worded note.

Dear Ellen,

I'm sending you this little gift to thank you for the many hours of enjoyment you've provided me with over the past several months. Our friendship has opened up many new fields of interest for me and made me realize how much I had missed by not having been exposed to the life of an artist. I'll never forget our time together.

But the time has come for me to move on. You must realize that I have a high degree of ambition and need to be free of encumbrances to pursue my interests. And of course, you understand that I've had and will continue to have a number of relationships with women, many of whom have much to offer that will to be to my future advantage.

I wish you continued success in your artistic endeavours. You can depend on me to put in a good word for you wherever I may have influence.

Goodbye and good luck!

Sincerely,
Teddy McCoy

By the method he had chosen, Teddy hoped to accomplish two things; first and foremost that rather than being simply heartbroken, Ellen would react with the fury of a woman scorned, thereby making the break quick and permanent. He expected that she might well drop by his office and hurl the bracelet at him; if so, that would move things along nicely. Or she might decide to sell the bracelet, pocket the proceeds, and write the whole affair off. Either way, it suited his needs. His second objective, one that I know he had not worked his way through very well, was that the brutal nature of the breakup and her reaction to it would put an end to his own emotional dependency on Ellen. A period of pain and unpleasantness would be just the medicine needed to put his mind at rest.

On both counts, Teddy was entirely mistaken and deeply disappointed in the outcome. His life experiences to that point had entirely failed to prepare him for a woman the likes of Ellen Bruce. She saw through Teddy's scheme as clearly as if he had spelled it out to her beforehand. She understood too well what made Teddy the kind of man he was, what he was trying to accomplish, and why he had chosen such a brutal instrument with which to do it. She recognized fear and panic when she saw it.

The dilemma she faced was whether to prolong Teddy's misery by begging him to reconsider, or to be merciful and let him off easily by quietly accepting his decision. What she was definitely not about to do was to give him the angry denunciation that he craved. On the other hand, she was also not about to accept his gift as some kind of cheap, insulting payoff.

Ellen thought the matter over for several days before taking any action. She saw no need to rush things. But there, she may have misread Teddy's state of mind. Teddy was anticipating an angry confrontation; or if not that, at least tears and perhaps pleading. He needed what he envisioned as a form of closure. When no response of any kind materialized, he became anxious, jittery, impatient, and querulous; he was finding it impossible to focus his mind on other matters while he waited for something—anything—to happen. His business partners were becoming fed up with his behaviour and they urged him to take a vacation to cool off and get his head straightened out.

When the day came that he lost his temper during negotiations over an important new contract and blew the whole deal, his partners finally had it out with him: whatever was bugging him had to be settled immediately, or their business relationship would soon come to an untimely end. And it wouldn't be on Teddy's terms, either.

Those fellows were not bluffing. Teddy could see no way of forcing the issue with Ellen; his only choice was to get out of town for a while. That would help to settle things down with his partners and, at the same time, get him physically far away from Ellen. He took a flight to Las Vegas, where he booked a room at a hotel for ten days and did his best to do the town and enjoy himself. The entertainment was lavish, the drinks were free at the casinos, and the women were pricey but plentiful, glamorous, and accommodating. It was the most depressing ten days Teddy had spent anywhere in many years.

What Teddy came to understand was that even if he succeeded in making Ellen hate him or even if he simply never met her again, he was unlikely to get Ellen Bruce out of his thoughts for a very long while. I believe that it was at that point when I finally began to become, ever so faintly, a presence in Teddy's consciousness. Our shared anxiety was providing a sort of meeting place. What I did not understand then was that the breakup with Ellen was the very earliest beginning of Teddy McCoy's downward spiral. I had no insight at all into what it might take to either break him or save him. Many years would pass before I came to understand that.

I discovered later that Ellen had intended to let Teddy think the matter over for a few days and then pay him a visit, not to reproach him, nor to beg for reconciliation, but just to return the bracelet as politely as her heartbroken state would permit, and hopefully part on good terms; such was the strength of her character. She was quite sure the relationship was over and was resigned to that. When she finally came to his office, she was told that he was away on vacation; the date of his return was uncertain. Teddy had purposely left hints with his associates that he was taking some other woman with him on his trip, a misleading bit of information meant for Ellen to absorb.

There was nothing to be done. She went away, wrapped the bracelet carefully and had it hand delivered to Teddy, marked "personal." All of this I came to know, bit by bit. What I discovered only much later was that the whole affair almost destroyed

Ellen Bruce; it was the only love affair that ever mattered in her life and it left her unable to work at her art for several years. When she finally found the strength to sculpt again, her work took on a much darker character, and it was rarely commissioned for public display thereafter. Most of it went unpurchased for the rest of her life. She never for a moment stopped loving Teddy.

Teddy McCoy and I, his resident spirit, have a great deal to atone for.

Moving Up

DESPITE HIS BUSINESS SUCCESS, TEDDY had never deluded himself that people in positions of power and influence liked or respected him. His humble and even disgraceful origins were public knowledge. People accepted him and cooperated in his schemes because it was to their advantage. He made himself useful. His boorish behaviour and obvious lack of education, his uncouth and brash style of dress, his crude street jargon, often punctuated with profanity, his questionable choice of companions, whether for recreation or business—all of this marked him for what he was: a ruffian of no consequence who had made good, but didn't really belong in polite company.

For the most part, Teddy cared little for their opinion of him. And yet he craved acceptance, if only because it would provide him with a better degree of security in his position. As it stood, he had to be constantly on his guard and he knew there would be many to rejoice if he should fail. He felt a need to change this picture in some way.

He decided that an advantageous marriage, preferably to "old money," would do the trick. He began to seek out and cultivate contacts with people who appeared to have both wealth and prestige, even when there was no immediate business prospect associated with the families or organizations concerned. He accepted every invitation to any social occasion or community event that looked promising. He especially sought to get involved in charity events and fundraisers, even though he was seldom generous with his personal donations; it was known that he had money to spare and he gave enough to encourage the organizers to invite him in hopes of receiving more.

I haven't mentioned Teddy's physical appearance until now, simply because such things are usually of no interest whatsoever to a soul. But the image he presented to those around him is meaningful within the context of this story. He was regarded as a decent-looking chap, not tall but very sturdily constructed, quick and graceful on his feet, a competent dancer, and a very proficient amateur boxer. His most notable feature, I suppose, was a full, thick crown of slightly curly light brown hair which appealed to women. On the other hand, his pale hazel eyes were so unremarkable and expressionless that many found it unsettling to meet his vacant stare.

Had he chosen to do so, I believe he could have been a remarkably successful professional poker player. The women who gravitated to Teddy did so on account of his brashness, his air of success, and the money he was prepared to spend when the mood struck him. He surmised that those attributes alone were unlikely to take him far if he chose to pursue the sort of woman he envisioned as his entrée into better circles of society.

He began to pay closer attention to how he was presenting himself; he selected a well-known tailor and took his professional advice more seriously than before. Flashy blazers worn over a golf shirt were gone, replaced by custom-tailored suits, fitted shirts, silk ties. He made an effort to tone down his speech patterns to better blend in with the crowd he found himself in. He wasn't entirely successful in upgrading his image, but at least the better-educated young women were no longer put off by his behaviour. He did his best to make himself agreeable to the young ladies he encountered at social events and went out of his way to be polite to their mothers. As for dealing with their fathers, he hoped that a credible business image would suffice.

It was at a hospital fundraising gala that he first met Moira Pascal, the only daughter of Gregory and Beatrice Pascal, heirs to a meat-packing fortune. Pascal had inherited his wealth, never had to work a day in his life. His wife, a depressingly snobbish society dame whose equally rich forbears hailed from someplace on the West Coast where they were in the lumbering industry, appeared to devote all of her time and energies to social engagements and various charitable events. As far as Teddy was concerned, they were both of them boring beyond belief, but their credentials and social status were ideal.

As for daughter Moira, Teddy would never have given her a second glance without her parentage. Well below average height, she was uncomfortably close to being considered chubby; her facial features, hair, and manner of speaking could all be summed up by the words plain and forgettable. She had been sent to all the right schools, where it appeared she had learned nothing of importance other than how to go about being the marriageable but totally uninteresting daughter of wealthy parents.

Although she had an older brother who was focused on making something of himself and would inherit the bulk of his parents' substantial fortune to assist him along the way, Moira also stood to inherit enough to keep her extremely comfortable for the rest of her days, even if she were to marry a pauper—a prospect her parents were determined to avoid.

But Moira was already nearly twenty-six and should undoubtedly have been married several years earlier had she displayed any features to make herself attractive. Teddy sincerely cared very little for her fortune other than for the prestige associated with inherited wealth; he considered himself capable of earning as much money as they would ever need.

As for her attractiveness, or to be more precise, her lack thereof, that also was of little concern to him. He was looking to acquire an icon, a living, breathing passport into the world of Toronto's social and political elites. Such an alliance had nothing to do with personal attraction, let alone sexual fulfillment. He did foresee siring a couple of socially acceptable children along the way; not that he bore any particular affinity toward children, but raising up one or two stalwart sons struck him as enhancing the image he sought to present.

You may regard all of this as terribly cold-blooded and even crass, and I will agree; but please stop to consider that precisely the same thought process is common enough among those whose primary interest lies in enhancing their social and economic status. An advantageous marriage has always stood on its own merit; prudence and social advantage overrule sentiment most of the time. Were it not so, there would surely be far fewer enticing mistresses secreted away by so many prosperous gentlemen throughout much of the world.

Ought I to have inserted myself into this campaign? If so, in what manner? And toward what end? We souls are not blessed with such wisdom. Logic and prior experience would have suggested that an alliance predicated on what were admittedly misanthropic motives was unlikely to lead to a state of marital bliss. But of course Teddy had other objectives in mind altogether. I could argue that his scheme was quite well conceived as a means of achieving the sort of upward mobility that he sought. And as for the possibility of my persuading Teddy McCoy to seek an entirely different objective? Not a chance!

Teddy's first and most noticeable asset in launching his courtship of this estimable young lady was his ability on the dance floor. Fortunately, Moira had also been schooled in that activity to the point of more or less overcoming any inborn awkwardness, the result being that they formed a reasonably attractive couple as he deftly piloted her around the floor. The parents were suitably impressed. In view of the daughter's otherwise few prospects, and encouraged by Teddy's careful control over his usual gaucherie, the Pascals were prepared to accept his obvious interest.

Over the next several months, as Teddy became a regular visitor to their home, the Pascals cautiously probed to determine the young man's intentions. Four months to the day after that first dance, Teddy presented an impressive ring in the presence of both parents and the match was struck. During that period, Teddy had kissed the lady five times and had never laid a hand on her person other than to hand her in and out of vehicles and sweep her around several dance floors.

The wedding took place on a clear spring day in the immense ballroom that took up a third of the main floor of the Pascals' Forest Hill home, with a lavishly catered reception in the formal garden, attended by several hundred of Toronto's well-heeled elite, almost none of whom Teddy had ever heard of, let alone met before. The honeymoon—a month-long, all expenses prepaid tour of Switzerland, Austria, and Germany—was one of many gifts from Moira's papa.

Upon their return, Teddy deposited his wife in a professionally decorated and luxuriously furnished penthouse apartment overlooking the Don Valley, and re-immersed himself in the business of getting rich. He had yet to discover whether he had succeeded in getting his wife pregnant, but he devoted himself assiduously to that endeavour; a few weeks after their return from the honeymoon, Moira paid a visit to her doctor, accompanied by her mother, and confirmed that Teddy could tick that item off his to-do list. Moira smoothly proceeded to assume the behaviour of a broody hen and happily migrated from almost chubby to just plain fat.

No longer needed at home for the time being, and still needing distraction in his determination to get Ellen Bruce out of his mind,

Teddy spent his days in aggressive pursuit of new contracts, and his evenings in the pursuit of a startlingly beautiful and shapely aspiring model named Leanne Arsenault. His selection of her for his attentions was not exclusively because of her plentiful physical allure; she was also part of his plan to alienate himself from Ellen. Leanne was well known in the local artistic community for her assignments as a nude model for artists and art students, especially sculptors; Teddy was sure that news of his liaison would find its way back to Ellen very quickly.

Whether Teddy's latest affair also became known to his *enceinte* wife didn't appear to concern him; and if Moira did know of it, she didn't acknowledge it. Her father certainly did find out, but made it clear to Teddy that he considered it a normal state of affairs. In his opinion, what a man amused himself with while his wife was otherwise "occupied" was none of the wife's concern.

I doubt if Gregory Pascal ever actually grew to like Teddy McCoy personally, their backgrounds being so vastly different; but Teddy's take-no-prisoners style of entrepreneurship appealed to the old man. Never having had to fight for his position in the business world, he seemed to derive vicarious pleasure from Teddy's exploits. He might have subconsciously viewed Teddy as a reincarnation of his own father, a man who had inherited a modest fortune and aggressively turned it into a much bigger one.

Over the years, Gregory had been handed positions on the boards of several corporations because of his wealth and connections, without having to actually do very much. Perhaps, from his perspective, the acquisition of such a son-in-law somehow legitimized his claim to being a tycoon, which he certainly was not. From the outset, Teddy's peculiar relationship with his father-in-law suited both of them.

For his part, Teddy was mindful to take full advantage of his new status as Pascal's son-in-law, inviting the old man to sit in on discussions of a major new project with the city. It was an ideal arrangement for both of them; Pascal had nothing to do but to show up and look dignified. And the first time Teddy asked Pascal to co-sign for a bid bond, far from being concerned about the request, Pascal was delighted to comply, thereby dramatically reducing the premium that Teddy was required to pay.

On the surface, all was well in Teddy's world; his business was thriving, and those who privately continued to question his legitimacy kept their opinions to themselves. But the breach of Teddy's emotional fortress that had been wrought by Ellen was not easily ignored. Neither his expedient marriage nor his ongoing affairs went any way toward repairing the damage. Teddy was no longer the entirely self-assured operator in dealing with women that he had been. A new awareness of his own emotional vulnerability did not sit well with him.

Ever since the breakup with Ellen, my connection with Teddy had begun to burgeon. His state of mind was gradually becoming more and more a part of my own reality, and he was beginning to sense my presence, even though my influence over him was still almost nonexistent. This continued to be a one-sided relationship, but I was no longer able to separate myself from his awareness, or to be a detached, silent observer. His inner turmoil was becoming mine. The two of us, each in our own way, were taking those first hesitant steps toward becoming *we*.

Respectability

I HAVE NOTICED THAT MANY prospective fathers, during the time when the scheduled birth is drawing near, become transformed from rational, competent adults into panic-stricken, helpless nitwits. Not surprisingly, this is most common among first-time fathers, finding themselves thrust into an unfamiliar situation where they can serve no useful purpose, but for some reason feel responsible for whatever might go wrong.

Such was definitely *not* the case with Teddy. He viewed the whole thing at arm's length, somewhat akin to monitoring the final completion of one of his construction projects. The only difference between this project and one of his contracts was that having been assured of the prospects for a normal birth, he anticipated receiving notice of a healthy infant, ideally a son, rather than a sizable cheque at the conclusion. In his mind, this anticipated birth constituted a minor milestone along his journey toward respectability.

As for me, apart from momentary consideration of what sort of background might be expected in the soul who was about to take up the task of assisting this new mortal during its perilous journey, I was becoming increasingly ensnarled in the complex emotions and upheavals that were progressively taking over the conscious mind of Teddy McCoy. We spent the better part of our waking hours on matters of business, punctuated by brief episodes of physical pleasure, and daily ritualized visits with Moira in the bedroom at home or at the birthing centre that had been lined up as the venue for this momentous event.

Teddy had gone to considerable effort to ensure that he would be kept very busy over the next few months, juggling two ongoing projects and aggressively pursuing another, to get working on it as soon as either of the current jobs began to wind down. By this routine, we (and I acknowledge my role in this) sought to push all thoughts of Ellen Bruce far into the background. In the interest of peace of mind, I did what little I could to encourage this tactic; but the one area of Teddy's life where I really could have a significant impact, his dreams, I had previously fouled up rather badly. Having once foolishly manoeuvred Ellen into that sphere, it was now damned difficult to exclude her; somewhat like trying to get toothpaste back into its tube.

I seek no forgiveness for my failings in this enterprise (such matters as blame or forgiveness having little relevance to me) but I hope you will be able to understand my predicament—and my rationale for what I did next. At that point, my primary goal was restoring Teddy's peace of mind. I could see only one way of relieving Teddy's conscious mind of the turmoil that he was experiencing: regret, loss, anger, and deeply repressed guilt. I perceived that it was necessary for Teddy to begin to resent Ellen and what she had done to disrupt his life. I needed to portray Ellen as an opportunist who had ensnared Teddy for her own selfish purposes.

Never mind your annoyingly mortal nonsense about fairness! That has nothing to do with all this. I had a task to perform, a mortal to escort on his life journey; the persona (and for that matter the resident soul) of Ellen Bruce was not my concern. If you're going to start lecturing me about human values, I don't see how I can continue with my story.

My campaign began with a series of dreams. Bear in mind that I cannot actually *create* dreams; that is a function of the human brain (one that I don't clearly understand, by the way). But I was able to manipulate scenes within Teddy's dreams, portraying Ellen as a scheming, shrewish character whenever Teddy's unconscious mind caused her to appear. My clumsy efforts were not very convincing at first, causing Teddy to awake in a highly confused state, unable to figure out what the hell was going on.

But eventually, we were beginning to recall Ellen's presence more with resentment than with regret. Teddy was never going to forget her, but I could foresee a time when we would be relieved that she was gone. Such was our state of mind and spirit on the day when Stanley Edward (not Teddy) McCoy was born, a robust baby with as healthy a set of lungs as his father had at that stage and (when he was not squalling) a placid pair of hazel eyes, the very reflection of Teddy's. In all other respects, the infant oddly struck Teddy as a miniature version of a very old man: red-faced, wizened, helpless, and unreasonably demanding of attention.

Once the initial excitement was over, Teddy was gratified to discover that his presence was once again unnecessary and irrelevant; anything he might have been able to do was likely to be a hindrance. Moira and the small circle of women surrounding her (Gregory had engaged a full-time nurse, who was intended to become a live-in nanny as befitted Teddy's new status as head of a prosperous upper middle class family) took charge of every detail. Teddy happily vacated the scene and spent his every waking hour engaged in his own pursuits. If he happened to fall asleep in the apartment occupied by a certain model, and failed to arrive at his own home until the following day, his absence was scarcely noticed.

Everything was proceeding according to plan. In due course, once Leanne Arsenault had served her purpose, Teddy stopped paying her rent, presented her with a generous parting gift, and sent her on her way. Being the sort of lady not troubled with romantic illusions, she bid him goodbye and embarked on a search for her next benefactor; there were plenty of willing candidates.

When young Stanley (who for some reason later acquired the nickname of Bud) was seven months old, Teddy decided that the time had come to advance his family project to the next step. He reverted to sleeping in his own bed every night, regardless of where he might have spent his evening; he intended to see to it that child number two would be coming along shortly. Before Stanley had acquired his nickname or celebrated his second birthday, he was joined in the nursery by a baby sister who was named Beatrice, after her maternal grandmother.

Gregory appointed himself Bea's guardian-in-chief and proceeded to monopolize her every available moment and spoil her relentlessly, over the strenuous objections of his wife and daughter. All of which once again released Teddy from any need to attend to family affairs, so he attended to his own. He found plenty to keep him occupied, as did I. After having made such a botched up mess of the Ellen affair, I was determined to do whatever I could to steer Teddy clear of another serious romantic entanglement.

A parade of amusing showgirls took care of that over the next several years, while Teddy consolidated his position as head of one of the most successful building contractors in Ontario, establishing a branch operation in Cambridge, which at that time was experiencing its own building boom, as businesses sought lower-cost premises well outside of Toronto, but still close enough to tap into the bigger market. The need for Teddy to spend part of his time with the growing Cambridge operation provided a legitimate opportunity for him to get away from Moira as much as possible. He acquired an extra girlfriend to keep him company in Cambridge, this time one who was, at least officially, married. With Charlene, there seemed to be no risk of a serious entanglement.

****

After the birth of Bea, Teddy saw no particular need for another infant; he declared that he was finding it difficult to sleep with

Moira, who was by her own admission a restless sleeper. He moved to a separate bedroom, when he did sleep at home, which was becoming the exception rather than the rule. Moira, for her part, had become increasingly fat with each pregnancy and offered no objection to Teddy's departure from the bedroom.

But even though she had always understood the role she played in Teddy's life, she seemed to resent being a showcase wife. We were finding her more querulous with each passing year, and we were relieved at being spared her presence most of the time. What sort of soul had taken up her cause I was never able to discover; she always struck me as somehow vacant in both personality and spirit. Nevertheless, over the years, she proved to be a tough adversary when it came to getting her own way.

Teddy took every available excuse to be away from the wearisome presence of Moira, especially when amplified by her mother. By her very presence, even by her frosty silences, Beatrice reinforced Moira's petulant behaviour. Conveniently, Teddy discovered an abundance of issues at the Cambridge operation that seemed to need his personal attention, often for a full week or more at a time. In the interest of gaining some measure of peace of mind, any excuse to be out of town made sense to me and I did whatever little I could to encourage it.

As his sojourns grew longer and more frequent, it seemed advisable to acquire a residence in Cambridge rather than continuing to pay hotel bills. And having a house of his own, if Charlene should happen to be arriving late and departing in the morning, there would be no nosy hotel staff to gossip about the matter. Not that her absentee husband concerned himself about the situation; Charlene had apparently run out of ways to provoke him into seeking a divorce, so far without success.

As for Moira, I believe she had long since stopped caring about Teddy's various liaisons. Relieved of the inconvenience of an unbecoming husband, she devoted herself to re-establishing her position in the social life of the city and supervising the upbringing of her two children in a manner that she and her mother saw fit. She had no difficulty tracking Teddy down whenever she wanted something from him. He leased a modest two-bedroom townhouse in Cambridge, adequate as bachelor quarters, and used part of it as his private office. About twice a month, or whenever a contract situation arose requiring his presence in Toronto, he shuttled back to the city, but he always contrived to be back in Cambridge within a few days.

While in Toronto, it would have been almost possible for Teddy to avoid contact with Moira altogether, except for his need to see his two children. I have some difficulty explaining that need and any discussion of it is likely to place Teddy in a very bad light. He hardly knew what to do with the little girl; while she was still an infant, he felt nervous holding her, as if she were somehow likely to be dropped and broken, like a piece of expensive china. Having never really lived in a regular family, fatherhood was an entirely new experience for him.

It was impossible for him to compete with the ebullient Gregory in that arena; the old man swooped the child up at every opportunity, teasing and tickling her, even finding it a great joke when she drooled or spit up on his shirt or her diaper happened to leak through onto his lap. By the time Bea was a toddler, Teddy's visits had become so infrequent that she barely remembered who he was. Teddy regretted losing touch, but he was unable to prevent that from happening; in the absence of any decisive action on his part to change the course of events, he gradually became like a visiting uncle, of scarcely any interest to the girl.

The issue with his son was a great deal more troubling to him. Teddy was determined to have a say in Bud's upbringing, and attempted to engage the youngster's interest by telling him stories about the world he lived in and knew so well—about building things, working with big machines, and dealing with important people. Determined to prevent Moira and the nanny (a person whose existence Teddy had never come to terms with) from ruining the kid and turning him into some kind of wimp, on the occasion of Bud's fifth birthday, Teddy presented him with a pair of skates, which of course didn't fit. He had neglected the logical step of taking the boy to a sporting goods store to be properly fitted.

A proper fit was eventually achieved, and Teddy did succeed in taking the boy skating a few times. Although Bud showed no real interest in learning to play hockey, as Teddy had visualized, he soon became a very competent skater (without any real help from Teddy, whose skill on the ice was rudimentary, at best).

When the day came that Bud, now seven years old, swept past Teddy on the ice, swung into a tight circle around him and executed a series of spins at high speed, Teddy found himself awkward and totally out of place. There was nothing he was going to be able to teach the kid and Teddy began to fear that the boy would turn into a figure skater. He tried to tell himself that there was nothing wrong about that. It didn't mean that the boy would become a sissy; but there was no common ground here, no contribution that Teddy could make. He and the boy had no shared vocabulary.

With each successive outing together, he could sense his hopes for any substantial relationship with his son escaping his grasp. Instinctively, he wanted to blame Moira for all this, but he knew better than to confront her about it; his objections to how the boy was being raised would just become one more topic of dissention, and one in which he was not going to be able to prevail.

****

Even though Teddy had lived all his life in Toronto, and was every inch a creature of that bustling city, at home in its elbows-out business environment, he began finding the atmosphere in Cambridge more and more to his liking. It was very much a high-growth centre and the construction business sector was almost as competitive as in the city, providing Teddy with ample opportunities to grow his business. The majority of the people he found himself dealing with, both as clients and as competitors, were a young crowd, recently arrived in the community. Most of the old-money people—families whose origins lay in one of the original towns of Hespeler, Preston, and Galt that had been amalgamated into a rapidly sprawling urban Cambridge—were not involved in the new developments. Teddy had almost no contact with the old guard at all.

Even though Teddy was still an outsider here, he was just one of many such; his questionable background, if anyone knew of it, was not an issue. Moreover, the business community, the local press, and the local populace in general tended to be more traditional in their outlook than in Toronto, rendering them less than sympathetic to labour activists. Being careful to stay well clear of local political activity, Teddy established arms-length but cordial relationships with several of the leading local politicians who were of similar mind. So whenever push came to shove on the labour front, most people sided with management. Unions were often placed on the defensive, a situation that definitely suited Teddy.

With a series of very successful contracts behind them, Teddy and his firm were becoming an established presence in the business life of the community. Having acquired a local address, he was invited to become a member of the Chamber of Commerce. The overall pace of life was decidedly less frantic than in Toronto. I recall Teddy explaining the difference to one of his partners, who was far from enthusiastic about doing business in a community he thought of as a backwater. "In Toronto, if I'm in a large building and have business to attend to a couple of floors up, I run up the stairs. In Cambridge, I wait for the elevator. But I still get things done and I'm not out of breath doing it."

For the first time in his life, Teddy occasionally felt comfortable knocking off work in mid-afternoon when it suited him. If

Charlene happened to be free for the afternoon, they might spend a few hours at one of the nearby conservation areas, going for a swim if the weather favoured it, or just indulging in a leisurely woodland hike. He tried his hand at golf, primarily as a means of improving his business contacts, but found the game far too fussy and exacting for hisliking; many of the men he met at the club took the game too seriously, turning it into just one more arena of constant competitiveness, the very opposite of what Teddy looked for in a leisure activity. If, instead of simple enjoyment, he would need to devote a significant amount of time, study, and effort into such an endeavour, Teddy expected payback; golf seemed to offer little beyond frustration and a feeling of inadequacy.

He became a frequent presence in the clubhouse and the bar, but never became a proficient golfer and rarely set foot on the course. Nevertheless, the time he spent at the club did pay him one significant dividend, in a totally unexpected way.

Although Teddy appreciated his newfound and more relaxed lifestyle, with none of his Toronto based partners taking an active role in the Cambridge operation, he was pretty much on his own from an operational standpoint. Negotiations with both his clients and his work crews, he handled personally, that being his own strength. He left the actual construction sites to a couple of hard-nosed straw bosses he had hired locally.

But having several projects at a time under way, that still left him with no one available to cover the somewhat grey areas of general oversight and logistics: project planning, permits, regulations, sourcing of materials and equipment, and so on; those were necessary activities that his two foremen disliked and seldom performed to his satisfaction. The smooth execution of these off-site tasks usually made the difference between a job that turned a healthy profit and one that gave him sleepless nights while barely breaking even.

Dealing with such matters day to day, especially technical issues involving civil engineers and architects, where his educational shortcomings could become troublesome, was not how he wished to spend his time. He found it difficult to recruit anyone with the level of experience and engineering knowledge to fill that role. A roughneck like Teddy himself, or a man who had come up from the ranks of tradesmen, lacked the technical knowledge and business acumen required.

With the intention of filling the gap, he hired a couple of recent graduates from the Building Systems Engineering course at Conestoga College. Both of them flamed out in short order because they couldn't cope with the rugged work environment, and because they clashed with his foremen, both of whom considered them prissy college boys and ignored anything such young, inexperienced men asked them to do. An area superintendent and project manager the likes of the man that his partners had recruited in Toronto seemed to be impossible to find in Cambridge.

One day, Teddy was having a quiet beer at the club. It was a drizzly day when there were very few people in the bar and no one out on the course; the sort of day that suited him because he wasn't likely to get dragged into buying an extra round by a bunch of guys who had already had one too many. An older gentleman, whom Teddy had met there once or twice before, attempted to engage him in casual conversation. Receiving a less than cordial response, the fellow remarked that Teddy looked like a man who had some problems.

Ordinarily, Teddy would have given such an overture the brush-off. Whether the brush-off would be polite or otherwise would depend on Teddy's mood at the time and the manner of the fellow, his appearance, and his tone of voice. But there was something out of the ordinary about this man, a lean, wiry guy in his seventies whose leathery hide proclaimed him to have spent his entire life outdoors, much of it in harsh weather and rugged working conditions. The sort of man who tended to gain Teddy's respect. He introduced himself simply as Logan; whether that was a given or surname was never quite explained and it didn't matter to Teddy.

What was soon apparent was that Logan had knocked about all over North and South America, working on drilling rigs, construction projects, shipyards, and remote encampments where the stakes were high and the environment unforgiving. Over the couple of beers that the two of them nursed over the next hour or more, they exchanged life experiences and Teddy revealed his dilemma about finding himself unable to recruit the kind of construction superintendent he needed.

Logan offered what he thought might be a solution. "You're not going to hire a guy like that off the street. Not around here, anyway. Men like that aren't available to be harvested full grown; you've got to plant the seed and grow them yourself."

"What the devil do you mean by that?"

"I mean, you have to find yourself a student enrolled in a co-op program at Conestoga, a fellow in his second year, when they start their on-the-job cycle. You know, these lads spend a few months in the classroom and then a few months working out on a construction project like yours, finding out what life on the job is really all about. By the time they graduate, they've made their mistakes and been kicked in the ass a few times, hard enough that they've actually learned something that makes them useful."

"I suppose that makes sense."

"But watch out! You don't want the top guy in his class or anything like it. You want a marginal student who works like hell just to pass the course and isn't afraid to get dirt under his fingernails and can survive a punch-up with a bad-tempered millwright. The kind of youngster who's likely to tell your foreman to get stuffed; and be ready to back up his words.

"Fellow like that will have learned enough in college to be useful for what you want, and he'll come with the right kind of attitude for the situation. What you want for starters is an unlicked cub. A guy something like you, if I don't miss my guess. I've run up against hard-asses like you in my time. I know the type when I see it."

"I guess I'll take that as a compliment."

"You can take it any way you like. I just call them as I see them and, at my age, nobody needs to take me seriously, anyway."

Teddy was never the sort to take advice readily, and he would have shrugged off this conversation, except for one factor: the background, personality, and mindset of the man who had given him the idea. Logan struck Teddy as legitimate, a man who had done the course, paid his dues, and earned the right to have an opinion. Teddy and I didn't manage to get to sleep that night until the paleness of dawn, with Teddy debating with himself the merits and feasibility of what he had heard that afternoon. I was hardly competent to offer an opinion on the subject, and Teddy was not likely to become aware of my opinion if I had one. But Logan had also impressed me as a man who ought to be taken seriously. I was hoping that Teddy's inborn stubbornness wouldn't hinder him from looking into the matter.

In the end, Teddy did investigate Logan's idea by visiting the placement officer at Conestoga, just to kick the tires, as he told himself. The current co-op class was well past the halfway mark of their second term, so it was too late in the year for Teddy to bring a student on board, but the college did arrange for Teddy to interview several of the promising first-year students to see if any of them looked like a good fit for the following term.

Those interviews convinced him of two things. First, that none of them, regardless of their knowledge, would be likely to last a week dealing with Teddy's foremen and crews. And second, that any one of them already knew more about the characteristics of concrete and the load-bearing capabilities of structural steel than Teddy himself had ever learned; but without the personality to cope with the work environment, their knowledge was of no use. He was discouraged to have been shown what looked like a solution, only to have it remain tantalizingly out of reach. The more he thought about Logan's advice, the more convinced he was that Logan was right. The very fact that it struck him as a great idea made it all the more aggravating. As far as I could see, we were right back at square one.

And yet, the notion refused to go away. Teddy could not let the matter rest. After turning the idea over in his mind dozens of times, to the point where I had begun to regret that the suggestion had ever come to light, Teddy recalled something important that Logan had said that day, causing him to consider a different approach. He visited the college again and this time he wanted to hear about first-year students who were struggling with their courses.

The placement officer wasn't at all keen to identify students who might be at risk of failing; such a thing wasn't likely to reflect well on the college. But Teddy wasn't easily put off, and he did eventually obtain the names of two students that were believed to be sincere and hard-working but were doing poorly their first year. Since this was in no way a potential placement as far as the college was concerned, Teddy just arranged to meet with each of them informally at a coffee shop, ostensibly for a chat about what life in their chosen field might be like. The first youngster appeared to be scared half out of his wits by Teddy's blunt style and probing questions that appeared to be more about his personal situation than his academic achievements. Their conversation lasted less than ten minutes.

The other young man was a different story altogether. His name was Tom Bunnett. A rangy youngster about twenty years old, well past the usual age for a first-year college student, he displayed a head of stringy, shoulder-length black hair, sallow complexion, and very dark, twitchy eyes that signalled "I don't trust you and I'm not about to take any crap from you!" The kid looked as if he hadn't had a square meal in some time, and his badly patched jeans and a checkered shirt that was two sizes too big—a hand-me-down or throwaway, for sure—betrayed his economic situation: flat broke and few prospects. This was the kind of youngster Teddy could easily relate to, and it took a remarkably short time for him to gain the young man's confidence. Sensing the possibility of some kind of casual job that might pay a good deal above minimum wage, Tom was more than willing to talk.

As bits of his story emerged, we learned that he was an aboriginal, a Delaware Indian who had more or less grown up on the Moraviantown Reserve in southern Ontario; at least, he had lived there until age thirteen when his stepfather, arriving home in a drunken rage, had slapped him around and then proceeded to beat his mother so badly that the kid had picked up a lacrosse stick and came close to killing the old man. That was when young Tom took off for the city, landing in Cambridge, where he had lived more or less on the street, picking up odd jobs until he had saved enough to pay for his first term at Conestoga.

The reason he was doing poorly in his course was obvious: he was working at two part-time jobs in order to eat and he had no regular residence, just crashed wherever he could find a spot out of the rain. All in all, he found it almost impossible to study. As matters stood, there was no chance this young man would be able to pass his first year. And yet it was clear to us that he was bright enough. Despite everything that was working against him, he was determined to graduate, partly because that would make him the first member of his family to obtain any kind of post-secondary diploma or degree.

The list of part-time jobs the kid had passed through was a woeful saga of substandard pay, abuse, and brutal working conditions. But to Teddy, those experiences told a story of survival. No construction site was likely to intimidate this young man. And he had shrugged off racial slurs all his life; for him, it was just an everyday reality of being Native in a white man's world.

Teddy McCoy was never a man who had difficulty making up his mind; and having once made a decision, nothing was about to stop him from turning decision into action. He made Tom an offer on the spot. "Just continue with your course this year, full-time study, no part-time jobs. Next year, you will accept whatever job I give you as your co-op placement. You will agree to stay with me for at least two years after graduation. I want that in writing from you. In return, I will pay for all of your college tuition, your room and board from today through to graduation, and $50 a week spending money."

The kid was dumbstruck. "Are you serious? Hell, man, you don't know me. Nobody gives an Indian a break like that. So, what's the catch?"

"No catch, son. Ask around; you'll soon find out that I don't bullshit anybody. And don't think that you can weasel out of the deal. If you run out on me, I promise I will track you down and you will wish you had never heard of me. One more condition, of course: you have to pass all your courses and graduate. So be ready to work your ass off."

"Geez! I still don't get it. Why me?"

"Very simple. You must want your education pretty badly or you wouldn't be going at it as you are. Secondly, if what you told me about where you worked is even half true, you're certain to be one really tough little Indian. And finally, I need a man who sees things my way and understands my business, a guy I can trust and who knows what he's doing. Recently, a fellow I have confidence in told me that I can't go out and hire such a man, that I have to 'grow him' myself. So that's what I aim to do. And you're it. So, do we have a deal?"

Ten minutes later, we had left the coffee shop and moved to a family-style eatery where Teddy gave the waitress his name, address, and credit card information and told her to bring Tom whatever he wanted to eat and keep bringing food until the kid couldn't eat any more. He gave Tom $50 cash and instructed him to appear at his office at 8 a.m. the following day to sign the agreement, after which he was to get himself a newspaper and go find a decent furnished room with meals provided. Teddy would settle up with the college for the rest of his tuition and costs.

Consequences

SO BEGAN A NEW CHAPTER in the life of Teddy McCoy. You may think that this represents a sudden shift in his personality. Not so. We've seen this sort of thing in Teddy before. It wasn't philanthropy on his part. He would have strenuously objected to being accused of a charitable act. It was simply enlightened self-interest, a way of getting what he wanted. But it also bears out another aspect of his character, his tendency to help people he perceived as receiving unfair treatment from the powerful. And there was one more factor that drove his decision. In Tom, he recognized a reflection of himself.

Tom Bunnett lived up to our expectations in every way one could expect—except for what was, at least for me, one troublesome issue. Tom had, at some point in his life, possibly the night he nearly killed his drunken stepfather, made up his mind to never again allow anyone to kick him around. He never went looking for trouble, but if someone pushed him a bit too hard, he pushed back even harder. Several times over the next few years, Tom got into brawls that landed him (usually along with one or more adversaries) in police custody. Teddy always went to bat for him, paid a fine, if required, vouched for his character, and never once condemned him for his behaviour. To the contrary, he insisted that every man has a right to defend himself. End of story.

Tom graduated with an associate degree in construction engineering, having served his co-op work time with STB, working on several of Teddy's projects. By the time he graduated, Tom knew as much about the business as Teddy himself did. There came a time when one of the foremen refused to take instruction from "a stupid Indian." Teddy was not told about this episode until some days later, long after Tom and the foreman had gone to the deserted back lot of a construction site and settled the matter between them in their own way.

Tom was back at work the following morning, bearing significant evidence of having survived a very rough evening. It was the better part of a week before the foreman was in shape to work, which didn't please Teddy because he had to leave a somewhat scatterbrained lead hand in charge of the site. There was never any further problem between Tom and the foreman and, in fact, having got each other's measure, they eventually became good friends.

The entire affair with Tom Bunnett was a valuable lesson for us. I came to understand that Teddy was blessed with a remarkably acute ability to judge character. By the time Tom finished his second full year at college and was preparing to return for his third term, Teddy foresaw that his investment was going to pay off, and he understood that making a similar investment in other worthy students who were disadvantaged was likely to pay good dividends. Never one to pass up on a good investment, Teddy made a point of meeting every first-year class in the construction courses at Conestoga about halfway through their term, looking for students who, like Tom, were struggling through no fault of their own.

Each year for the next six years, before leaving the Cambridge operation and returning to face growing issues in Toronto, he sponsored one or two students, based almost entirely on his assessment of their potential and their character. Every one of them graduated and went on to successful lives, although only two of them actually remained with STB after their obligations to Teddy had been fulfilled.

I found it significant that the college hierarchy never approved of Teddy's approach, considering his selection of students arbitrary, and possibly unfair to others not selected. He was never publicly acknowledged or thanked for what he did for those students. Such are the workings of institutions. Sometimes appearances count for more than results.

Teddy couldn't have cared less about the college's opinion. Ever the self-styled "cat that walks by itself," he disregarded the opinions or actions of those having no hold upon him. His mindset was, of course, a deliberate strategy meant to prevent the attitudes and actions of irksome people from consciously affecting him. That is not to say he was oblivious to them; he simply chose to ignore them. Whenever someone sought to exert their power over him, he took action to address the issue on his own terms. For example, the impossibility of living in close proximity with Moira, he had dealt with by simply getting out of town and establishing himself elsewhere. Conforming to others' views was never his concern. Pacifying his internal demons, however, was quite another matter.

Apart from Ellen Bruce, Teddy's liaisons with women had always been of such little substance that they never disturbed the calm waters of his inner certainty. Such emotional detachment had the distinct advantage of making it easy for him to drop the latest woman out of his life and move on. On the other hand, none of those affairs were of the slightest help toward putting Ellen out of his mind, or even relegating her to some sequestered backwater of his consciousness. Taking up with Charlene had failed to become more than a momentary diversion.

As for my clumsy efforts at discrediting Ellen by gerrymandering his dreams? My campaign had succeeded only in sowing confusion in Teddy's mind. He was still faced with a dilemma for which nothing in his experience had yet prepared him: the awareness of having made a monumental error, a life-changing decision that had taken him far down a path from which he could not retrace his steps. His own stubbornness had enabled him to deny that fact for a long time; but it was the uncomfortable reality of his synthetic marriage, an alliance that had complicated his life without having achieved its purpose, that finally broke through his denial.

Nothing he (or I) could conjure up was likely to transform the persona of Ellen Bruce into something she was not. Her presence stalked his dreams as relentlessly as did his recollection of her face, her walk, her voice. More tellingly, it was her sheer vitality, her honesty, the force of her uncompromising personality that refused to let him go. On my part, having abandoned all hope of casting Ellen as an opportunist, a schemer, I was relegated to the role of an impotent observer of Teddy McCoy's nightly torment. The inescapable knowledge of his own failure did not make him a congenial companion for me, and it rendered him even less forgiving of the failings he saw in those around him.

Over the nearly seven years that we spent largely in Cambridge, I had hoped that a more benign set of surroundings would eventually round off some of Teddy's jagged edges. Even though he failed to form friendships there, he at least didn't accumulate new enemies. His off-and-on relationship with Charlene never amounted to much and they eventually just lost interest in each other and drifted apart, never having had much in common to begin with. I continued to reach out to him to the degree that I could, largely through his dreams into which I inserted snippets of pleasant scenes from some of my past "lives."

The Cambridge operation was profitable, and he was personally accepted in the community. One might have said, with some justification, that all was well. But in fact, Teddy was a very lonely man. It was not emotionally possible for Teddy to acknowledge (even to himself) that his life was empty, lacking in any real fulfillment. He therefore declared himself to be successful, and no one ventured to contradict his assessment. But, in fact, the best part of being in Cambridge lay in what was *not* there, namely Moira, the rest of the Pascals, and Teddy's never-ending confrontations with local politicians, competitors, and the media in Toronto. Wherever Teddy lived, he would never be able to leave the spectre of Ellen behind.

In due course, the Cambridge hiatus had to come to an end. Trouble had been brewing in the partnership. When business had been going well, it was easier to smooth over disputes; but as their position in an increasingly tight market became harder to maintain, long-standing resentments were becoming disruptive.

Duff Simon had gradually turned most of the day-to-day ironwork business over to his son, but he still exercised a strong influence on how business was to be conducted. His insistence on integrity in dealings often clashed with a couple of the other partners. And now that Jack was married, with a growing family, he and his father shared a deep concern for the longevity and reputation of their business. They were determined to be able to pass on a strong family business to the next generation. They believed that some of the questionable deals the partnership had been putting together were putting their long-term objectives at risk.

Teddy's style of doing business remained as aggressive as ever, but the degree of respect that he had developed for the Simons usually caused him to take Duff Simon's complaints seriously. Teddy attempted to apply his deal-making skills to mediate between the partners, not always with success.

Matters were also coming to a head in what was left of his marriage. Teddy was compelled to deal with the situation and he could not do that from out of town. It suddenly occurred to him, rightly or not, that he had in effect been hiding out in Cambridge as a means of avoiding issues he didn't know how to resolve. Such a notion was intolerable to Teddy's image of himself as the indomitable, take-charge, opinions-be-damned man who made excuses to no one. He abruptly turned the Cambridge operation over to his now-well-prepared deputy, Tom Bunnett, bought his way out of the lease on the townhouse, and returned to Toronto full time.

The primary bone of contention between Teddy and Moira centred on the education of the two children. Moira and her parents had seen to it that both children were enrolled in exclusive private schools, a move that Teddy opposed, feeling that it would just make them into useless, prissy, privileged social climbers, the sort of people Teddy had always despised. Surrounded by such a bubble, they were likely to become complete strangers to him. It was impossible for him to prevail in the argument because the plain fact was that Teddy was father in name only; he was seldom at home and when he was at home, he found it difficult to deal with either child in a fatherly way.

The disagreement really became bitter when Bud, as he was then called, turned eleven, ready to move to junior high school. Without even discussing the matter with Teddy, Moira made arrangements for Bud to enrol at Upper Canada College, a truly elite school. In that environment, the boy was certain never to establish any sort of rapport with Teddy. Already, they were becoming distant figures to each other, finding little common ground or shared interests. Teddy had always envisioned a future where he would take his teenage son round to his various construction sites and impart to him an understanding of and appreciation for real work. He wanted to be able to show him off to his partners and clients, teach him about the realities of bidding and negotiating contracts, dealing with trades people, and, above all, about living and thriving in the real world of men; men who worked hard, got their hands dirty and backed down from no one.

That was a battle Teddy could not win. And his relationship with the Pascals, who had backed Moira on her stand, was damaged beyond recovery. Their only concession to Teddy was that two Saturdays per month, Bud would spend the day with Teddy. He saw the whole thing as a de facto divorce, which it essentially was. An end to the marriage had become inevitable. Up to that point, at least on the business front, Gregory had continued to back Teddy financially where necessary, even though by this time Teddy rarely needed Pascal's active support. He did, however, continue to need Gregory's name and endorsement.

Any time Teddy chose to ignore the generally accepted rules of enterprise if it suited his purpose, Gregory was still onside—as long as Teddy's tactics were successful. Gregory Pascal was not a man who troubled himself a great deal about moral issues for their own sake. But when, as was inevitably going to happen, Teddy encountered some serious blow-back from those in positions of authority as a result of his questionable bidding practices and strong-arm dealings on the labour front, Gregory found himself in an increasingly uncomfortable position. His image as a life member of the old-boys network could be put at risk, a prospect that he was unprepared to contemplate.

That, along with the dispute about the boy, left Gregory and Teddy on opposing sides from which they were not able to return. Alienation from Gregory did not bode well for Teddy's future career in a city where everyone he dealt with knew his whole story, including where he stood with the Pascals.

****

By the time Bud turned fifteen, he and Teddy were rarely in direct contact and their infrequent visits invariably centred on demands or complaints, most of which had been initiated by Moira. Gregory and Teddy had become awkward, antagonistic aliens to each other. He and Moira had permanently separated, although neither wished to seek a divorce. Without Gregory's visible presence, Teddy was finding it increasingly difficult to deal with anyone in authority at city hall.

He and his partners were still landing plenty of commercial work and the business was certainly profitable, but government contracts of any kind became almost unobtainable. His old enemies were openly challenging his legitimacy, honesty, even his competence as a major contractor. The respectability that Teddy had bought with his marriage had proven ephemeral.

I wonder if I've conveyed to you how isolated Teddy had become at the age of fifty, how austere the emotional landscape in which he lived. Here was a man who had never experienced ordinary friendship. Consider that for a moment.

Unknown to him were the carefree, playful, raucous antics of schoolboy chums; the rambunctious, comfortable give-and-take typical of comrades in midlife; or the sympathetic affirmation of lifelong friends acknowledging their failing faculties in old age. The person Teddy McCoy lived with, spoke with, debated with every waking hour, was Teddy himself. By continually reinforcing such a stunted model, I had to wonder if he had gradually begun to like himself less and less as the years passed and the walls that he surrounded himself with grew thicker.

If ever I had been engaged with a host who needed a source of refuge, a quiet place, a welcoming pair of arms, this was the one. What was needed was not another lawyer, another enforcer, another spin doctor. What Teddy needed was to be surrounded by people who had no agenda, were not waiting to be paid off, whose loyalty had no price tag. And he needed supporters who would tell him the truth with honour and without fear. But was this man prepared to listen? I was becoming a presence, but one that Teddy, the conscious man, the lifelong combatant, seldom chose to heed.

Above all, what Teddy did not need right now was to accumulate more enemies, as he had done time and again over much of his life. The art of forming friendships required the kind of forbearance, patience, and trust that Teddy had failed to develop. All of his life experiences had taught him to take the initiative, demand results, and trust no one.

In response, I sought to insert a vision of loyalty into his imagination, whether in dreams or awake. Whenever he dreamed of success, I conjured up steadfast supporters who would applaud him. When he perceived threats, I offered stout defenders at his side. But every step along the way, I was struggling against Teddy's reality. Something fundamental would have to change within Teddy McCoy himself in order for our narrative to change direction.

Trouble at City Hall

FACED WITH SEVERAL POWERFUL ENEMIES on city council in Toronto, Teddy's instinctive nature as a fighter and an outsider came to the fore. By shaving their bid prices to levels barely above break-even on all the work available to them in Toronto, while subsidizing their bottom line through more profitable work in Cambridge, Teddy's company, STB, was exerting increasing economic pressure on their Toronto competitors; this at a time when there was a temporary slowdown in growth around the Greater Toronto Area.

Janus Builders, one of the other major contractors, had become over-extended and was finding it difficult to stay afloat. Seeing an opportunity, Teddy offered Janus a "lifeline"; it was ostensibly a merger but in fact a takeover at a distressed price, an offer that Janus couldn't refuse. To make the deal a bit more palatable and with the intention of presenting a favourable face to potential customers, the original president of Janus Builders was left nominally in charge of the Janus portion of the merged enterprise. Janus and STB pretended to bid against each other, to create the impression of competition, but the ploy fooled no one. The two builders always decided in advance which of them would win a contract and placed their bids accordingly; and one of their two proposals was always priced so as to undercut any other competitor.

Competing contractors, encouraged by a couple of hostile local politicians grateful for an issue that might divert attention from their own incompetence, publicly accused STB of bid-rigging. But there was nothing demonstrably illegal about the whole thing and Teddy ignored all the noise that was being made. Meanwhile, with construction work in decline that year, Teddy played hardball in negotiations with the trades. He maintained his own private non-union crew on standby, ready to step in if one or two of the trades became too difficult to deal with. That sent a strong message to all the others. Teddy found relatively easy work to keep his own crew occupied when there was no regular work for them and he made sure their families were well looked after, even providing summer camps for their kids at no cost.

Even I, despite my full access to what was going on in Teddy's complicated life, couldn't exactly figure out how he came up with the funds to pay those fellows; being a soul embedded with Teddy's conscious state of mind did not make me into a financial whiz. In some instances, Teddy's sources of income would not likely have stood up well under public scrutiny and I saw no advantage to paying close attention to a matter I could not possibly do anything about.

If you consider that a cop-out on my part, so be it.

The atmosphere in and around the construction industry was becoming increasingly poisonous. In addition to labour disruptions and brutal competition for contracts, contentious issues having to do with permits, workplace safety, zoning, and so on were arising with increasing frequency. Fires on building sites have always been a risk, mostly due to the somewhat chaotic environment, with fuel and lumber in close proximity to welding and heavy machinery, along with limited fire-control capability. I doubt if the frequency of fires around that time was any different from usual, but with builders and politicians both being in a combative state of mind, a couple of unexplained blazes became big issues in the local media. Insurance companies were getting nervous, and rates for fire coverage were rising rapidly.

The fire marshall was being hounded for answers, and when sparks from one small fire at one of STB's sites set off a blaze at a small shopping mall across the street, Teddy's enemies demanded action. Teddy shrugged the matter off as routine noise, and it appeared at first that the matter would go away as soon as the local media found something else to occupy their attention and fill in the half-hour during the suppertime TV news.

But then, a much bigger fire erupted at STB's most hostile competitor's main worksite, almost completely destroying a fifteen-storey apartment building that was near completion. During an interview, Philip Lewis, one of Teddy's adversaries on city council, hinted broadly at arson and suggested that the activities of certain "other major contractors" ought to be looked into, even though there was no evidence whatever to support such a claim.

This was the sort of thing that lawyers relish: angry people with deep pockets, further encouraged by political noise and media attention. Teddy and his company initiated a libel suit and demanded that Lewis issue a public apology, resign from council, or preferably both, failing which a multi-million dollar lawsuit would proceed. The councillor refused to back down, and lawyers on both sides prepared to do battle in court. The local newspapers loved it.

Gregory Pascal, aghast at his family being associated with Teddy's growing problems, finally compelled his daughter to seek a divorce. He publicly disowned his son-in-law and even pretended that he and his wife had opposed the marriage in the first place. Although no one really believed that, opinion about Teddy's conduct was so negative that the old man's claim was not publicly refuted.

Teddy, of course, had far more urgent matters to contend with than anything having to do with a long-dead marriage. The

Pascals could not possibly be of any use to him any longer, so he didn't contest the divorce, other than to stipulate that he would continue to have unrestricted access to his son, now sixteen years old. And in view of the Pascal family's wealth being many times greater than his, he offered Moira a nominal alimony of $1 per year and $100,000 in child support. To his dismay, Moira refused the offer, demanding that Teddy be given no access to either child, and seeking alimony of $200,000 plus escalating child support, an amount still to be determined based on need.

None of this was going to do anything toward making Teddy McCoy a better person. His conscious persona and I were clearly going to be facing a fight on several fronts. I had no option but to do my best to support him, keep him sane, and do whatever I could to calm his mind, allow him to sleep, and keep him thinking logically. Matters had long passed the point where some accommodation could be worked out between Teddy and those acting against him. During some of my past lives, I had learned a good deal about various kinds of warfare—military, legal, and otherwise; I was, to some degree, prepared for what we were about to face together. All-out warfare was soon under way.

Every fibre of Teddy's personality favoured attack. While legal battles were about to begin on two fronts, Teddy opened up a third front: he very publicly announced that he would be backing the campaign of a long-time crony named Vicente "Vince" Donato to unseat Philip Lewis in the forthcoming municipal election. Donato ran several prominent businesses in the sprawling Italian community, where he was the local go-to guy; he had personally financed the building of a community centre and soccer pitch in Little Italy, and he was widely respected across the city, especially in immigrant neighbourhoods, where he had actively opposed city regulations concerning zoning and street commerce, regulations that many recent immigrants saw as discriminatory against newcomers.

Teddy stated publicly that he would finance Donato's campaign to the maximum allowable by law and that he would be personally calling in some favours from many quarters to help boost Vince's campaign. The newspapers immediately predicted that Lewis was likely to lose badly; he might be better off to drop out of the race and devote his time and energy to defending himself against Teddy's libel suit. Lewis stated that he welcomed an opportunity to "expose that crook, Teddy McCoy and his shady friends" for what they were.

Lewis raised the ante by questioning how Donato had managed to obtain a building permit to triple the floor space at one of his properties, despite that project having been contrary to local zoning; he also mentioned that Teddy's company had done the construction and that their application for a variance had been supported by several city politicians who were known to be friends of Teddy McCoy. This war was quickly growing wider and uglier.

What was happening in the tempestuous life of Teddy McCoy was, on an individual human scale, not materially different from the great conflicts that characterize all of human history. Understandably, humans condemn war and widespread mayhem, disruption of societies, and dislocation of populations. I share that view, but I also have the advantage of a broader perspective, a longer view of the cycle of time.

Regrettable as it is, I perceive that war actually serves a useful purpose within the overall context of human existence. Of course, you disagree, so please allow me to explain what I mean by that.

War preserves diversity by setting disparate groups—races, cultures, religions, etc.—at odds with each other. They arm themselves. No single tribe gains total ascendancy, at least not for long. Even when one powerful individual and his circle of supporters gains absolute power over a territory and its population, potential challengers always remain—internal, external, or both. The downfall of the powerful is constantly being plotted. This obliges both the oppressor and the oppressed to remain vigilant, aggressive, and adaptive to new threats and changing conditions. The species remains strong; it is never allowed to become fat and complacent. Nor does one dominant individual or tribe ever succeed in ruling the entire earth; woe betide the human race if that should ever occur.

In the midst of conflict, individuals succumb; the race survives and even flourishes. At least, it has done so until now. Whether the species will ultimately succeed in destroying itself remains to be seen. Likewise, it was unclear whether Teddy McCoy and his allies would be strengthened by the coming conflict or be swept away in it.

The Crash

WHILE MOIRA'S DIVORCE PETITION WORKED its weary way toward an as yet unforeseeable conclusion, the municipal election roared into full operation. Those running for seats on council coalesced into two warring camps: those who saw the complex relationship among developers, contractors, planners, and the municipal administration (both elected officials and salaried staff) as a practical working arrangement that enabled things to get done with limited hassle (they were generally, although not officially, in Teddy's camp); and those who perceived the existing regime as corrupt, pernicious, and self-serving (they were vehemently opposed to Teddy and everything he stood for).

To some degree, the election had turned into a referendum on whether or not Teddy McCoy and all those who chose to do business with him should be thrown in jail (or even better, according to some, lynched).

We were somewhat bemused that our exploits were considered to be of such monumental importance to the community. But, of course, we understood that politics is a high-stakes game and one where participants are liable to suffer serious wounds that may cripple them permanently and deprive them of not just elected office but their reputation, livelihood, even their self-respect, sanity, or life itself. There were, as Teddy had suggested, many in the community who owed favours to him; there were others about whom Teddy held knowledge that they could ill afford to have made public.

Heavily financed by his circle of supporters, Vince Donato ran a vigorous campaign. Despite a continuous barrage of accusations of wrongdoing from the Lewis camp, the immigrant and ethnic vote held strong. It was a close race, with Donato winning his seat on council by a margin of less than 1 percent of the vote. We joined in the Donato team's celebration at the biggest Italian restaurant in the city. The next day, Lewis demanded a recount and launched an investigation into voting irregularities, claiming intimidation, vote-buying, bribery; everything short of ballot-stuffing.

The accusations and demands would not go away, but Lewis failed to gain official support for his accusations and Donato was sworn into office, along with two other candidates who were friendly to him. City staff were not very bold in opposing proposals from Teddy's company and with new support on council, STB quickly picked up two minor but lucrative new contracts on city projects. Before work could get under way, STB was faced with potential work stoppages; new demands by several trades were escalating rapidly. The unions smelled a badly wounded opponent, one they had long resented.

Having spent virtually all of his ready cash on the municipal campaign and on lawyers to pursue the ongoing libel action against Lewis, Teddy was also faced with major legal costs in his divorce case. Under his present financial stress, he could not afford to lose that battle with Moira. Needing to start work on the municipal contracts right away so as to start generating income, he had no choice but to agree to the unions' demands, thereby turning two otherwise profitable jobs into break-even, at best. Any minor mistake would tip the work into loss status.

The divorce proceedings dragged on for nearly two years, at the end of which Teddy came out a winner—at least in theory. Moira's alimony demands were rejected on the grounds that she was not in need, whereas Teddy was, by that time, teetering toward insolvency. He also was granted unrestricted access to his children, since the Pascals were unable to demonstrate any wrongdoing on his part.

That too turned out to be a hollow victory, since Bud, now eighteen and about to graduate from high school, was heading to university in England, and made it perfectly clear that he wished to have nothing to do with his father whatsoever. As for Bea, Teddy would not have had the first idea about what any conversation with her would entail, nor did he care. He was left with no family connections, no public credibility, and more debts than his limited income could sustain. Both of his lawyers had quietly begun to write off most of Teddy's unpaid bills.

And then, one of the claims of electoral irregularity that had been launched by Lewis finally bore fruit; a discontented former employee of Vince Donato went to the newspapers with a story to the effect that Teddy had bribed him and some of his friends to vote for Donato. That accusation encouraged several others with various grievances to come forward with similar stories (some, but not all of which might have been true). Before long, the trickle of accusations grew into an avalanche. Donato was suspended from office pending a more thorough investigation, and half a year later he resigned altogether.

Teddy quickly found that there was no one at city hall who would even discuss business with him. It became pointless for his company to prepare a bid for city work. The rival contractors that he had routinely beaten on proposals in former years were finding it easy to underbid him in his financially stressed state. His long-time loyal non-union crew was no longer available to be brought in to work on construction jobs and reduce his cost, because he had been obliged to stop paying them. They remained his allies,, but they needed to get paid, so they had taken jobs elsewhere.

I never became an integral participant in Teddy, the entrepreneur, but I had become very much a part of Teddy, the increasingly lonely and troubled private man. We suffered together as one, our outward bravado completely failing to fool anyone or to relieve the dismal reality of an inner life that had become increasingly bleak. Externally, we were surrounded by enemies and internally there was no respite, no peaceful corner into which the conscious man, the sleeping man, or the resident soul could take comfort.

Lacking the exhilaration of success on the business battlefield, having in the end failed in our relationships with women, lacking friends and soulmates, we were becoming terribly isolated. That very isolation was what enabled both Teddy, the conscious man, and I, his resident soul, to finally merge into a shared reality. For Teddy, it was not like becoming aware of a *presence*; rather, it was like coming to understand a part of his own personality that he had previously been unaware of or had perhaps repressed. In a tranquil state of mind, this awareness of the soul can induce a state of euphoria and provide the host with the confidence and strength that is integral to peace of mind.

But such tranquility cannot be achieved by the mortal person by himself, regardless of what else is going on in his life; the soul must be able to do its part, deliver its quota of spiritual resources to the relationship, and in this I acknowledge my own deficiency. My store of spiritual strength that had been built up many years back during some successful lives had ebbed in recent times. I know that I let Teddy down when he needed me most.

That is one reason I feel compelled to tell this story: to confess my failings and try to explain what came of that and what I did about it. What I've been trying to demonstrate is that despite all I've told you about Teddy McCoy, he really wasn't such a bad person, just a player who had been dealt some bad cards in the game of life, and played the only way he understood. More to the point, he was a fellow who was stuck with a soul that didn't always live up to its share of the bargain. I wasn't providing strong enough spiritual support, and some of my choices of tactics were ill-conceived and not well executed. Our situation was deteriorating, and I needed a better game plan.

In an endeavour to offer some ray of optimism, I permitted Teddy to half-consciously glimpse some happier aspects, a few pleasant scenes from a couple of my former associations with men who had led more successful lives many years back.

One of my earlier hosts, Olin Kern, had been a highly respected landowner and merchant in what was then called Upper Canada. That man's remarkable courage in the face of public censure, his refusal to be cowed by the political bullies of his day, his resourcefulness, and above all his astonishing generosity of spirit, combined to make my time with him one of my most treasured experiences. It occurred to me that possibly just a tiny bit of Olin Kern might somehow be saved, tucked away, and with patience shared with Teddy McCoy; an echo of Olin's strength of character might somehow sustain us both in this trying time. If I've once been a hero, prevailed against daunting odds, achieved exceptional things, surely I can be such a man again! The qualities that sustained me then must surely be there to sustain me now.

It's doubtful if this ploy on my part was much help to Teddy, the conscious man, since the sensation, as Teddy experienced it, of having lived in a different time among different people felt like a pleasant but essentially pointless daydream; and it failed to offer me any way out of our current dark state. Looking back on this now, I view the whole thing as a bit of idle tinkering that I'm not proud of. As a general rule, revealing former lives to your host seldom enriches the host's life experience. It often causes confusion, and in extreme cases may even cause the host to question his own sanity—especially if he tells other people about his experience.

Conscious denial rings hollow and offers no peace; the hurt we pretend to shrug off, the loss we discount, the guilt we repress:

none of that ever goes away. Teddy had always sought to rationalize his phony marriage as a prudent strategic alliance. His rejection of Ellen's love was simply something he had to do, for the good of both of them. His brutal destruction of Howard Silver was just business—nothing personal. But what about my failure to do one damn thing about it? Surely that was just my weakened state limiting my effectiveness. Or was that really the case? Had we just found it too convenient to make excuses for our failures?

Teddy had never found himself living within the constraints, the legends, the overarching structure, and the attendant aggravations of family. That missing ingredient had rendered Teddy somewhat directionless. By that, I mean that in order for a man to get along toward where he thinks he's going, he needs to have some sense of where it is that he's coming from. Family is a point of departure. Despite all its heartbreak, all its frustration, family provides context.

My journey with Teddy had become a journey from nowhere and consequently not a journey at all—just a series of stopovers. Usually, when a man reaches for much and fails, his family is there in the background; they may be condemning the injustice of all that befell him—or, on the other hand, reminding him that he ought to have remembered where he came from, that he overreached and got what he deserved. Should he be successful, there may be cousins who, though envious, will hasten to seek his favour. He will learn that neither their pique nor their praise will change his fate. Their applause has not smoothed his path, nor will their resentment impede him, and if he's wise, he will shrug off both.

But their presence is part of his reality; if they are absent, his picture is incomplete. Teddy had been obliged to create his own place in the world, a task that he had not fully accomplished. Context is a part of meaning, that elusive thing that humans instinctively seek. As do souls. Only very late in our sojourn together did I come to understand that it was the discovery of that meaning that was our true mission.

Over my many past life engagements, I've learned that the course of human events often resembles an unrehearsed drama; when things are going badly, they frequently take an unexpected turn for the better—or a great deal worse. Our turning point came on a blustery Friday when we were supervising the placement of a crane at a construction site, a crane that absolutely had to be in place and operational so that work could get under way on Monday.

Everyone present knew that it was too windy that day for such a job, but the project was already running late; permitting a further delay for lack of lift capacity was out of the question. The supervision of such an undertaking would normally never have fallen to Teddy. This was Jack Simon's territory, but Jack, a man whose family always came first, was at the bedside of a very ill daughter. We were standing in the exact spot where Jack would have been, for the best view of proceedings. Would the whole thing have been attempted at all that day if Jack had been in charge? We can never know.

I have no precise knowledge of such mechanical issues. I only understood the significance of these matters by way of what went through Teddy's brain about it and listening in to the loud imprecations of the riggers that Friday. What I do know was that there was one horrendous crash and a shriek of tortured metal as a truss swung sideways and buckled and a 60-ton counterweight fell twelve storeys to the ground, reducing a dump truck to a crumpled waffle. Bricks, panels, and debris that were swept off the building by the broken truss flew in all directions in the gusting wind.

I, of course, do not feel pain, but I suffer along with my host because I cannot separate myself from his trauma. At that moment, we suffered no pain, because Teddy lost consciousness the instant that both his legs were crushed and a foot-long splinter of steel severed his left kidney. I knew, however, that pain was on its way and plenty of it. I also knew that everything in this shared life of ours was about to change, and certainly not for the better.

****

How can I possibly convey my state of spirit over those next few hours, totally helpless to do anything whatsoever to support our cause? Waiting for Teddy's consciousness to emerge following the emergency surgery that removed the destroyed kidney, amputated his left leg above the knee, and made the first tentative steps toward reconstructing what remained of his right leg, I recall entertaining the ludicrous notion that Teddy's career on the dance floor was over; as if that somehow mattered now! How could this man, whose vitality depended so critically on his self-image as the indomitable, spit-in-your-eye street fighter, possibly function as an invalid? What was to become of us now?

I made a promise to myself when I set out to give this account, that I would endeavour to tell the truth as best I understood it, whether it reflected well or badly on me; so I will confess right here that for a time I found myself regretting that Teddy's life did not end when the crane fell that day. Without doubt, my sojourn would have been a great deal easier. Looking back on it now, I understand that it's better that souls have no say in such matters. And I believe that had Teddy perished that day, our story would not have amounted to much and I would probably not have found it nearly as compelling to be sharing it with you now.

There's no particular reason that souls should be spared the suffering that mankind has to endure. We both contribute to bringing that suffering about by our own imperfections, our own bad choices. Immortality has not granted any of us perfection. Even if we should acquire a bit of wisdom along the way, we don't necessarily make the best use of it.

As the physical aspect of Teddy drifted up into an awareness of where he was, I was immediately overwhelmed by the state of confusion that ruled our shared conscious mind; I had no spiritual resource that I could call upon to allay the shock and horror that took over. In this situation, the mortal man and the awareness of his desperate state, overpowers the spirit; there is no room left in that constrained sphere of existence, the inescapable reality of *here* and *now*. At such a moment, immortality counts for nothing.

Teddy had only a vague recollection of the falling crane, but even before he was fully awake, he understood that his left leg was gone. Anything beyond that had not become at all clear, but surely that was enough. I became aware of a sound that began as a groan and erupted in a howl of anguish having nothing to do with physical pain, a terrifying noise that brought a nurse running almost instantaneously, with a sedative at the ready. Even so, it was too late to prevent Teddy from descending into shock. He lost consciousness, leaving me to wait and ponder how I was likely to fare, whether, in fact, I would be of any help at all in the struggle to come.

It occurs to me that, despite our entirely different existence from that of mortals, we souls share some of the frailties, if not outright foolishness, that you people are afflicted with. In my case, one of those weaknesses is a tendency to whine about my situation. For much of this narrative, I've griped about my host's intransigence. That my task would have been so much more straightforward if only my host had been more… what? Receptive? Kind-hearted? Sociable?

But at this point, this crisis, I had come to see things more clearly, that complaints were a lot of nonsense, lame excuses—even wishful thinking, an exercise no soul has any business indulging in!

The crash had jolted me into a realization of where I had been for the past fifty-four years; that I'd had the unique privilege of a life entirely spared the humdrum, the routine, the captivity that the majority of modern men endure. The emasculating millstone that grinds the wage-slave, the corporate man, the bureaucrat. The misery of the tradesman who detests his task, the academic who loathes the stupidity of his students and the pettiness of his colleagues; in short, the day-to-day drudgery and inevitability that tomorrow will be no different from today because he's trapped.

Such men, and they are legion, know in their hearts that they cannot change their fate—or have conceded that the price to be paid for breaking the cycle is more than they can pay. Their only means of surviving is to repress their frustration, convincing themselves that all is well, that they are successful in what they do. They celebrate each small victory, each notch they advance in their chosen field. Many of them acquire spouses who help them to create a wished-for reality by supporting and applauding their accomplishments. An accumulation of material artifacts—a fine residence, a healthy salary, perhaps a summer residence by a lake, a luxurious holiday now and then—all of that stuff helps to push aside the unsettling knowledge that they're trapped within a system and its rules.

The tedium that afflicts the wage-slave has been described as soul-destroying. That isn't really accurate from my perspective; a soul cannot be destroyed. But enduring such a fettered life along with one's host can certainly be burdensome. I've been there more times than I care to recall.

But despite the many challenges that he had to face, even the failure of his marriage and all his recent financial setbacks, my host had never suffered under that suffocating regime so many men endure. No employer, no institution, no authority had ever succeeded in keeping Teddy McCoy captive. He had always found ways to escape, to set his own course; and he willingly paid the price of doing so. In most cases, he had even negotiated the price downward in his favour. He was without doubt a free man. I cannot recall any host in my past who made as few compromises, accepted as few limitations, and feared as few of his fellow men as did Teddy McCoy.

But today, all of that had changed. Teddy could not rebel or bluff his way out of this, could not negotiate his sentence. From this day forward, he would be held captive within his damaged body and, at the same time, his economic options had also vanished. The game now had rules that Teddy had never before accepted. There was also nothing that I could do to change this narrative; I, too, had to accept a new reality and with our abrupt loss of freedom, I understood for the first time what a unique and exhilarating journey I had been on until now.

A soul is not granted the privilege of grieving. I had no choice but to accept my host's current and future state and make the best of it. Another thing we souls have in common with mortals is that no matter how vast our memories are, we cannot see into the future. I believe we all, both souls and mortals, should be grateful for that.

****

Over the next three days, with patience and skill, the medical staff brought Teddy slowly back into a state of awareness and comparative calm. Horror alternated with grief and foreboding at what was likely to come. As soon as he was deemed sufficiently stabilized, he needed further surgery in an attempt to save his remaining leg. What I feared most was the onset of depression, despair, even resignation. But there I misjudged; regardless of his condition, those were not to be contemplated, not for Teddy McCoy! What emerged was rage; and a degree of rage that I'm sure the hospital staff would gladly have traded for a dose of depression.

He lashed out at everyone and everything and soon became notorious as the worst patient the staff had ever endured. He shrieked, cursed, shouted, struggled to rise from his bed, and had to be physically restrained from dismantling his bedding, tearing off bandages, tubes, monitors. The soul finds it difficult to cope with rage because it becomes unreasoning. I could only wait for it to subside. Then the question would be: what would come next?

What followed was neither acceptance nor despair. As Teddy migrated in and out of consciousness over the next two weeks, while a succession of excavations and adjustments were carried out on his right leg, transplanting pieces of flesh, cobbling bits of shattered bone together into something resembling a femur, his rage descended into seething anger, resentment, and sheer determination to prove that Teddy McCoy was not about to be defeated. His treatment of those who were struggling to help him was frankly disgraceful. Their patience in the face of his tirades and imprecations was astonishing.

One of his partners visited him the first day that he was coherent, but was met with curses, as Teddy vented his rage upon anyone within shouting distance. There was no possibility of any discussion about the state of affairs at the work site, let alone any consideration of his future prospects. Once he had settled down considerably, all four of his partners came—I suppose to reduce the volume of abuse that any one of them would have to endure, simply by spreading it around. That day, Teddy's sheer strength of mind was astonishing to me, despite having gained such intimate knowledge of his character. As if he had calmly thought the matter through, which could not possibly have been the case, Teddy coldly informed them that he was bowing out of the partnership.

"You guys know damn well that I'm no use to the company now. I'll just get in the way. And I can't stand the way you look at me! I will not tolerate your pity, got that? Just get hold of an accountant to figure out how much the business is still worth; can't be very much, given the state of affairs. Then you just buy me out. I know there's no cash right now, so just give me your IOU for whatever my share is worth, and you can pay me off later when things recover. And I'll hold you to that, you bastards. Never think you can weasel out on me. When I get on my feet, I'll…

"Say! That's a laugh, ain't it? I don't even have one foot that works yet! Anyway, never mind. Teddy McCoy isn't dead, which means that I *will* get you bastards if you try to jerk me around. Now, don't try to argue with me. I'm in a hell of a lot of pain right now and all I want you to do is get your sorry asses out of here! Now, just go!"

And they left. They had no choice. And so, the next phase of Teddy McCoy's career began.

I hardly need to mention that the ensuing struggle was hellish on all fronts. From the hospital, Teddy was moved to a rehabilitation centre, remaining there full time for a couple of weeks, then he was sent home to a penthouse apartment that he no longer needed and certainly could not afford. He spent three half-days each week at rehab while he was fitted with a temporary prosthesis, a clumsy thing that he was never able to stand on, let alone walk with.

He was not eating, and he was losing weight. His eyes took on the glazed look of a man in a fever, even though his temperature was normal. In less than a month, he was back in hospital with an infection that refused to respond to any of the antibiotics they tried. The mangled right leg developed a whole series of new infected areas. His one remaining kidney was hardly able to cope with the combined attack of infection and aggressive medication. His anger continued to boil.

Three of Teddy's old Clan members went to the penthouse, quietly packed up his personal belongings and moved him to a much cheaper apartment, leaving the expensive furniture behind. The rent was four months in arrears and the landlord, faced with no good options, just sold the best furniture to cut his losses. Teddy was essentially broke, so it wasn't likely the rent in his new place would be paid either, but at least the hospital had someplace to send him to if he ever kicked the infection.

The corruption investigation that had been launched by Lewis dragged on through the summer months, making life extremely difficult for Teddy's former partners, but not worrying Teddy at all; it was just one more thing contributing to his anger. By this time, there was nothing much they could do with us financially; he had not been well enough to get on with declaring bankruptcy, a move that was inevitable.

Lewis was determined to gather enough ammunition for an indictment on criminal charges of fraud, bid-rigging, and bribery; chances of making any of that stick were remote, but Teddy and his former partners could get dragged through the courts, which would permanently destroy what was left of their reputation and business prospects, even if the whole thing were to eventually fizzle out. Teddy's lawyers would lose out on their fees, but being lawyers, they would recover their losses elsewhere.

Despite his bravado with his partners, the chances of them ever being able to pay Teddy anything were fading by the day as their business dwindled and failed. As Teddy had told them to do, they obtained an assessment of the present value of their business and gave Teddy a lien set at one fifth of that value. Before the end of the year, it was doubtful that Teddy could have been able to sell that lien for a tenth of its face value. He never tried.

Despite being finally and permanently out of business, we still received a daily newspaper, *The Globe and Mail*; and Teddy read through the business news every day. I suspect it had something to do with nostalgia. That was how we learned that STB Contracting had been dissolved, each of the four remaining partners walking away with nothing. Or at least I think three of them left with nothing. I have no way of verifying anything about it, but it seems to me that Duff and Jack Simon must have somehow retained their personal integrity and their belief in themselves. But their days as the only aboriginal-owned company in Canada erecting high steel were gone. Among all our regrets about how things had turned out, that loss was one of the hardest to accept.

After four more sessions in the hospital, the infections were finally brought under control, and we found ourselves in a woebegone one-room walk-up flat on a drab little street off Roncesvalles, with nothing whatever to do. The polyglot neighbourhood, best described as no-collar rather than blue-collar, had taken us full circle, back to the sort of place where a feisty, full-of-beans teen-aged Teddy McCoy had first established himself in the pool halls and back alleys.

Late into the night, after the noise and bustle of the city had subsided, we were comforted by the familiar rumble and screech of streetcars making the turn at the junction, a sound so deeply buried in Teddy's past that it would have intruded on his wakeful awareness only if its irregular but inevitable repetition had somehow ceased for some time, like a clock that had stopped ticking. In a way, this was a setting where Teddy belonged, where he understood the rules—and where, in the impetuousness of his youth, had often made up his own rules.

But all that was a lifetime ago. Being a self-employed contractor, Teddy was not entitled to any kind of compensation for his injuries, and had no insurance coverage for the cost of the endless stream of drugs needed to battle infection. He had lost a third of his original body weight. He was fifty-five years old and looked like a sickly man of seventy. It occurred to me that while the accident hadn't killed Teddy, there wasn't much left of us to kill. What no one could kill was Teddy's anger, his determination to fight on, regardless of having nothing left to fight *with*. It was no longer clear to me whether we had anything left to fight *for*.

And through it all, there was no escaping the personality that was Teddy. The song of a man's youth never really fades away entirely; it just changes shape. The pace of the heartbeat that began in the womb may vary and falter, but the fundamental rhythm persists until the moment when the resident soul departs. Therein lies destiny, if such a thing exists.

****

Teddy had always been "good press." His colourful exploits and many battles had often provided the local media with plenty of material. On a slow news day, there's nothing as enticing as a bit of slander and muck-raking to fill columns and sell newspapers. One local reporter, named Jason Fitch, recalling the glory days when Teddy McCoy had been front page news, saw an opportunity to profit from Teddy's downfall. Becoming impatient with the lull in activity, he badgered Philip Lewis for new information on his charges against Teddy and his partners. Lewis, being in a foul mood, told Fitch to go and talk to Teddy or just to go to hell if that suited him better. Fitch took Lewis's advice and went to see Teddy, who was happy to oblige.

Fitch arrived well prepared, with a tape recorder, notepad, and, knowing Teddy's preferences, a bottle of Scotch. Not having met Teddy in person since the accident, he was deeply shocked at the emaciated specimen that greeted him at the door of the apartment. Being a journalist with sound instincts for unearthing the human drama underlying a news story, Fitch probed for an understanding of what kind of man Teddy McCoy had become, what drove him, how he was coping with his demons. He also discerned that Teddy seemed to be living mostly on black coffee, pizza, and Scotch.

After an hour of wandering conversation, none of which Fitch recorded, Teddy was getting visibly tired and increasingly impatient, so they agreed to resume the interview another day. When he arrived for a second session, Fitch omitted the Scotch and brought a couple of takeout chicken dinners instead. Fitch was not a generous man, but he was probably worried that his subject might well fail to outlive the article he planned to write; keeping him well-fed and reasonably sober seemed like a wise approach. If that didn't get him what he sought, he was prepared to revert back to the whisky.

The piece Fitch wrote reported that Teddy was preparing to reopen his original lawsuit against Lewis, accusing him this time of criminal harassment in addition to libel. When asked how he intended to finance his case, Teddy had told Fitch that an old friend—a lawyer whose career had first taken off due to business sent his way by Teddy McCoy—had offered to pursue the case on a contingency basis. That statement was not strictly true, since what the lawyer had actually agreed to do was to pursue the suit in retaliation if and when Lewis failed to make any of his current charges stick.

None of this, of course, was imminent, but it made for a good story and Fitch was happy to encourage Teddy to keep it going as long as readers were interested. It also provided Teddy with no income or prospects of income but it satisfied his need to fight back. His anger and antagonism were the only things keeping Teddy McCoy alive.

Forgiveness

A FEW DAYS AFTER FITCH'S piece was published, there was a knock at our door, a rare occurrence these days. Our abode was a lonely one: no family, no friends. People stayed clear of us with good reason. An aura of bitterness and resentment is unlikely to attract casual visitors. Assuming that it could only be one of Teddy's many creditors hoping to extract some payment, however small, against the amounts owing, we took our time answering the knock. But knowing that the creditor would have to go away disappointed and being determined not to hide from reality, Teddy opened the door.

The elderly man standing there bore no resemblance to any of the dozen or so people we had expected to see. We didn't recognize him at all, and yet there was something about him that suggested we had encountered him before somewhere; perhaps many years ago—or was I just being reminded of someone from one of my previous lifetimes? Foolish idea! We stared at each other wordlessly for some seconds and then the man simply said, "Hello, Teddy. It's been a long time. May I come in for a moment?"

"Do I know you?"

"We used to know each other quite well. You needn't be concerned. I don't want anything from you. I gather that there are a lot of people who are wanting something from you these days, but I'm not one of them."

That voice! An unsettling jolt of recognition, an echo of the past, followed by something previously unheard of in the implacable mind of Teddy McCoy: panic. The soberly dressed elderly man standing calmly in our doorway was none other than Howard Silver, the man whose business, whose reputation, whose very life Teddy McCoy had destroyed more than twenty years back. Surely, he had come to gloat over Teddy's downfall. And yet, there was no hint of malice in his voice or his bearing, nor did he appear in any way gleeful as he beheld the wreck that Teddy had become. Teddy was lost for words; the two men continued to stare at each other for some moments.

Finally, "Of all the people I might have expected to meet today…"

Still no response from Silver.

"But why? What in God's name brings you here?"

"I've come to offer you something, if you will accept it. It will cost you nothing and it will help an old man like me sleep better at night. Might I come in and sit down for a moment? I suffer from arthritis and I find it difficult to stand for very long."

"Alright, come in, if you must. But I still don't understand."

As soon as Silver had settled in a chair, he said, "Thank you. I'll be brief and I know you're not likely to have become a patient man. My reason for being here is simple: I've come to offer you my forgiveness for what took place between us. And to acknowledge my own foolishness that played a part in it. I ask you to accept this from me and I ask nothing more from you. I'm an old man and I've not been well. My days are numbered. I don't want to die with this matter unresolved between us."

"But how can you possibly…? I don't get it. What am I supposed to do about all that now, after all these years? Don't you understand that I haven't got anything now, any means to do a damn thing about it?"

"Of course. That's exactly the point. I've waited until there's nothing that you or I can do to harm or help each other. So we're quits. The case is closed."

"I… I don't know how to… That is, I don't know what I can say."

"Just consider what I've said. I'll go now. I understand that this has been a great shock for you." And he rose and made his way to the door.

As he stepped into the hallway, he left us with this: "Perhaps we could meet one day for a cup of tea. Or something stronger, if you prefer. It might help us both to have a quiet talk, compare notes. It appears that both of us have seen far better days. We have at least that much in common."

And with that, he was gone. Teddy was left stunned, immobilized. He was a man who had looked into the abyss and beheld his own ghost staring back at him, a man who had just suffered a life-ending defeat. He sat unmoving on that beaten-up old armchair for perhaps the better part of a half-hour. The turmoil in his mind was unlike anything I had ever experienced with him. And then, he did something that I had never thought to see; he fell forward, his head almost in his own lap, and he began to weep.

The one thing that he could not face, the one thing that might in fact finally break Teddy, overwhelm his anger, rendering him helpless and lost, was Howard Silver's forgiveness. Teddy had no pattern, no strategy, no mindset, no comprehension to enable him to cope with this. An attack of any sort, or curses and denunciation he could have shrugged off. Vengeful ridicule at his sorry state he could have responded to in kind. But forgiveness? Acceptance? Kindness? For that, he had no answer; and it was likely to break him when nothing else ever could.

What sort of creature was likely to emerge out of what was left of Teddy McCoy? I had no idea.

At that moment, I also understood that whatever became of Teddy, I was inescapably a part of it; there was no space left between us. I found myself completely diffused with his devastation and my own state of shock and confusion had become real in Teddy's consciousness. For the first time, mind and soul had merged into one. I was now Teddy, body and soul.

What transpired over the rest of that day and several days that followed remains a blur now. I recall that we became very drunk, a state in which I had never before truly participated; before that, whenever one of my hosts became inebriated, I observed the situation very closely, but not personally, if that makes any sense to you. This time, we drank, slept, woke again, wandered from living room to kitchen and back to bed. We drank until there was nothing left in the house to drink. We drifted. And when we could no longer drink or sleep, once again, we wept. There was nothing else left for us to do.

I don't recall how many days passed. But eventually, hunger (another sensation I had never before truly appreciated) compelled us to do something to keep body and soul together. One thing I was certain of: under no circumstances were we prepared to let this body die. Not now. We had to see this thing through together. We had to figure out what the hell was supposed to happen to us now.

There were still a few dollars left in the wallet, money that no creditor had yet found a way to extract. To keep on living, we needed to eat. So, miserable and hung-over as we were, we found our way to a cheap diner a couple of blocks away. A place that stayed open late, a haven for shift workers too exhausted to cook at home. It also attracted a variety of artists, musicians, and mostly out-of-work actors, largely because the roast beef dinner on offer there was the cheapest in the whole city.

I guess it must have been almost midnight when we got there, found a quiet corner, and ordered the specialty of the house. A loosely connected stream of the usual habitués began to drift in, apparently a group of people who had emerged at the end of some show nearby. We tried to ignore their busy chatter. And that's when the second blow struck, the one that I doubted we would survive.

We became aware of a presence beside our table. A pair of low-heeled shoes at the lower extremity of a pair of tailored slacks. Women's shoes and slacks. Obviously not the waitress, because she, for convention's sake, was one who chose to torture her feet with heels. To take in the rest of this person and discover why she was standing at our table required the raising of Teddy's eyes, which also meant facing more light than was comfortable in our current state. But whoever this was would not likely go away unless we acknowledged her presence and did or said something to make her leave.

And there she stood. Ellen Bruce. Now well along in middle age, a bit grey at the temples, perhaps looking a bit worn, but unmistakeably Ellen.

It was at that very moment, after having accompanied so many humans on so many lives, that I finally understood, in person, with full force, the pain that love can bring. "Take My Breath Away." Is that how that song goes?

"So here you are, Teddy. I wondered if I might run across you in this neighbourhood. I understand you've moved… down a bit."

There is nothing that I can say. Why is she here? Why now? This woman was out of my life! Why bring her back after all this time? Whose demented idea was this?

"May I sit down? You appear to be alone this evening."

Of course we are! How else could we satisfy this miserable body's need for nourishment for ten bucks?

"Oh, Teddy! I'm so sorry. Please don't try to stand. I heard about your leg, so did everyone. I didn't mean that to sound so horrible, about moving 'down' into this neighbourhood. It's just me being bitchy… and you never used to be easily offended by my jibes; I just thought… Oh, I don't know what I thought. I just saw you sitting here all by yourself, looking so damned blue."

Is this real? Is she just a trick of my addled imagination, sent to torture me? No, it's no trick. She's here, sitting across the table from me. What now? Damn it, Teddy. Say something!

"Ellen…"

"Yes, it's been a while, hasn't it? None of the standard clichés work, do they? 'How've you been?' 'What's new in your life?' 'You're looking well.' Somehow, none of it seems to apply. And please, for the sake of whatever honesty either of us still pretends to honour, don't try telling me that I haven't changed a bit.' It seems to me the years have not been kind to either of us."

"Ellen, I don't know where to begin."

"Then don't. Let's just sit here and breathe. Anything either of us says will be wrong, anyway."

So there it is. It's almost as if both of us have been in a time warp for the last… What is it? Twenty years? No, a lot more than that! And never mind all those years! She looks wonderful! Strong, self-assured, genuine, not a fake bone in her body, and look at me: a washed-up physical wreck without two nickels I can call my own! What could I possibly say to this amazing woman who once loved me… to her great sorrow!

I find myself wishing I could still separate myself from Teddy, be the wise, cool, detached soul, playing with his mortality, messing with his dreams, unaffected by the reality of his torment. But that's all past now. Teddy's pain is my pain. I put us into this situation, now it's all part of my reality. Our reality.

"I recall asking you once why you bothered with a roughneck like me. That seems to have been a prescient question, looking back on it now. All I ever brought you was grief. I guess it's my turn to indulge in the clichés. So… how's your life going?"

"I think you're better informed than you let on. You know that I don't do public art anymore. Truth is, the movers and shakers don't really like what I do these days. I can't blame them. And, no, since you know better than to ask, there isn't anyone else in my life. How's that for frankness? You always said you appreciated frankness in me."

"I didn't ask..."

"No, you didn't."

"I'm sorry..."

"Don't be. Look, I honestly didn't expect to find you here tonight, and I wasn't planning to ambush you. But I can't deny that I'm glad to see you. That's all I can admit to you and to myself. Couldn't we meet somewhere and just... talk? I can't just walk away without us having the chance to... I don't know... perhaps understand where we're at. Could you drop by my old studio?"

It takes us a long time to figure out what we could possibly say. Words! How utterly useless. What does she expect from us? And how could we possibly meet any such expectation? We burned every damn one of those bridges a long time ago. Best to leave bad enough alone. We grasped for some diversion, some device to hide our misery, our inadequacy—yes, damn it, our guilt! A hoodie of anonymity, denial.

"Ellen, you know that all I'm likely to do is screw up your life."

"Too late for that, my dear. That's just us. It's what we do. I reach out for dangerous enterprises that can't work, noisy toys that blow up in my face. And you? You dish out big, ugly doses of reality. I should know better than to expect anything different."

"You're right. It is too late, so why would you want to open up all that painful history? And why now? Don't you understand that I'm all washed up?"

For some time, neither of us spoke. It might have been less than a minute, or it could have been hours. Who knows? A thousand notions, memories, arguments, scenes, wishes, regrets, things that might have been or never could have been cascaded through our consciousness. Excuses. Stupid reasons we dreamed up or forgot to dream up for what had happened or should have happened. None of the poise, the purported wisdom that this soul ought to have acquired over an unremembered number of lives was of any damn use to us. All that was left here was just stupid, ham-fisted, combative Teddy McCoy, lost and bewildered, totally out of his depth.

Finally, she stood up to leave. "You are such a fool, Teddy. The only thing you ever needed to know about me is that I loved you. Heaven help me, but I will love you until the day I die, regardless of what destruction that brings upon either of us. You know where I live. There's nothing else I can say."

I've no recollection of how we found our way back home that night, but we must have done so because that's where we awoke much later.

****

Misfortune, failure, and condemnation could not knock Teddy McCoy down. Those are only setbacks, at worst; perhaps they are even opportunities for new ventures. But forgiveness, undeserved, thrust upon him, with no merit on his part? This unmanned him altogether because it was totally outside of his control. It was an uncalled-for act of grace, one that left him helpless, lost for direction, unable even to make sense of his past, let alone find his way forward. For Teddy McCoy, an act of surrender was unthinkable and in accepting this gift, he found himself finally broken, at the mercy of whatever was to befall him now. A fighter functions only as long as he continues to fight. Fighting is all that he is. He lacks the ability to not fight. When he cannot fight, he ceases to exist. The individual who was Teddy McCoy had simply… gone.

How can a man live if he comes to despise the person he has always been? What becomes of him if he finds himself trapped in the persona of a man whose entire system of values, beliefs, objectives, habits, and urges is suddenly revealed to have been false? When I was just a fellow traveller, an almost impartial observer, a cool strategist seeking ways to influence my host's behaviour, I had found it at times frustrating to be swept along in Teddy McCoy's destructive career. But it was not painful. Now the entire situation was different. There was no longer any *he* and *I*, just *we*.

This spirit was in many respects just as ragged as its host. Like two hikers lost in the wilderness, we had met and joined forces, but together we were as helpless as each of us had been on our own. Neither of us were finding our past selves the least bit likeable. Was it perhaps advisable to do away with both of them? Or was that even possible? Where do you go when you reach the end of the road you've been travelling and you know that you cannot turn back?

I had never found Teddy to be as deeply depressed, defeated, as he was at this point. Once before, when Teddy was under attack from all sides, I had pulled back a curtain, so to speak, allowing him a glimpse of experiences from lives I had shared long ago, hoping to reinforce his confidence in his ability to rise above the adversity of the moment. I cannot say whether that ploy had been of much use to him; but once again, I seemed to be running out of ways to support him and I needed to do something. This time, instead of simply revealing a personality and related events to him as if what had occurred was his own memory of a past life (a risky thing to do) I undertook a different approach.

One of my former hosts had become a British admiral during the Napoleonic wars. While he was still a captain, assigned to a staff position under the most illustrious admiral of his day, he had fallen in love with an uneducated young woman of humble background. Despite being an honourable man with a strong moral compass, he was nevertheless highly competitive and ambitious to rise in his naval career. In that extremely class-conscious environment, he understood that marrying a poor girl with no family connections would be a hindrance rather than an asset. Despite my efforts to influence his decision, he abandoned his love and married the daughter of a cabinet minister, a move that was helpful in his eventual promotion.

But the marriage became a horror story, and he came to deeply regret his actions. In the end, he resigned his commission, faced down his domineering in-laws, divorced his wife, and resolved to seek out his former lover. A highly fictionalized version of that man's story had recently been made into a film. In real life, the retired admiral never succeeded in reuniting with his lost love; but, of course, the Hollywood people couldn't have the story end that way. I was struck by the parallels between that series of events and Teddy McCoy's life, and realized that there was a relatively low risk way to share that past life with Teddy.

Over the next week or so, by persistent suggestion, I convinced Teddy that he needed some diversion, subtly directing his attention to an ad for that movie in the newspaper he still read almost every day. It took a great deal of effort, but by repeatedly getting him to notice the ad, I influenced him into going to see the movie. When I revealed to him what I had experienced long ago, he experienced it not as if it was his own memory of a past life, but rather as if he was just recalling a film that had seemed unusually real and relevant to him.

I was confident that this experience would be helpful in Teddy's recovery, since, in the film, the retired admiral succeeded in overcoming the strictures of the society he lived in, was re-united with his lost love, and died happy. But my ploy failed because what Teddy came to remember was not what happened at the end of the film; I had revealed too much of the real story. Teddy came away convinced that the people making the film had got it wrong. I had hoped to bolster Teddy's resolve; instead, he remained deeply troubled about his past decisions and could see no clear way forward. Once again, by my ineptness I had failed my host. Saving Teddy was going to depend on Teddy himself.

****

Anyone who has survived extreme trauma discovers that the only choice available is to go forward, no matter how abhorrent that prospect may be. All of Teddy McCoy's schemes had ended in total failure; we could not bear to contemplate carrying on in similar fashion. There was nothing to be gained by doing so, and we had no desire to achieve any of the goals that Teddy had once aspired to. Many a philosopher, sage or mystic has been known to refer to a critical juncture in life as a crossroads. But here was no real crossroads that we could see, because there did not seem to be any left or right; it was a dead end. Was it time for the soul to abandon ship, for this mortal to give up the ghost? How quaint those old expressions seem! And how distressingly apt!

Let me for a moment step out of this scenario and once again become, just for the sake of telling this story, that same smug soul that I introduced you to at the beginning; able to observe, to comment from a safe, comfortable vantage point the struggles of my mortal host. Might it not be prudent to simply write this whole episode off, persuade this unpleasant McCoy fellow to do away with himself, set the spirit free, and begin all over again with a clean slate? Of course, the idea is tempting. But to be honest, giving up is just a cop-out, an admission of complete failure. Such an option will not satisfy that aggressive mortal Teddy McCoy nor is it acceptable to this troubled spirit that finds itself stuck with him. For both of us there is only one possible choice: find a new road.

Now that Teddy and his soul were completely united in one being, I finally understood that the power of forgiveness had at last changed Teddy by breaking the cycle that had driven these two entities on the path we had taken together. And now the love of Ellen Bruce was no longer an obstacle, an encumbrance to

Teddy's life plan. It was a miracle, a thing of unimaginable beauty to be treasured.

But because of its immense value, it was also a thing to be approached with fear and awe, not because it was fragile and likely to shatter if dropped—after all, it had already survived cruelty and neglect. Our fear was of failing to live up to it; the risk of being found unworthy. And in our case, there was damn good reason for that fear, having already performed so miserably, treating that love so shabbily—and all for the most disgraceful of reasons: greed, hubris, and falsehood.

If we were going to find that new road, the journey was likely to be a difficult one. We had dug ourselves into a terribly deep hole, filled with pestilence and misery.

First step to take? Stop digging!

Redemption

EMBARKING ON A NEW LIFE at the age of fifty-five, ill, crippled, and broke, is a daunting prospect. The first thing it's certain to teach you is humility. There's the encouraging fact that almost any move you make is likely to be an improvement over your former state. That said, you have to become accustomed to making small steps. There is no room for hubris. And accept the fact that no one who knew you before is going to trust your motives or cut you any slack now. You've got to earn every gain you make, often several times over. The journey is not for the impatient or faint of heart. Because of your notoriety, should you claim even the smallest victory, you are sure to find yourself under attack. In fact, the world you lived in before has not changed, so you may well be under attack no matter what you do.

The first really steep hill for us to climb was learning to accept the forgiveness of those we had wronged; not because forgiveness was earned, but simply as an act of grace. After our life of conflict, as experienced by Teddy McCoy, and after my own troubled former spiritual journey, we were ill prepared to accommodate acts of forgiveness or kindness with both confidence and humility—virtues that may at first appear contradictory but in fact need to coexist.

A sober inventory of our remaining assets was not at all encouraging.

Financial resources? Nil.

Reputation? Dodgy.

Friends? None.

Next of kin? Alienated.

Bodily strength? Shot.

Business prospects? Scanty.

Strength of spirit? Questionable.

On the positive side of the ledger, the business acumen we had once possessed had surely not vanished. Surely, the energy, drive, and resourcefulness that had enabled Teddy McCoy to rise above the disadvantages of his youth had not been completely lost.

But to find that new road, perhaps none of the old Teddy McCoy chutzpah would be of much use. It was those very characteristics that had conspired to knock us off our horse; a quite different set of skills would be needed now, and learning to apply those skills was not going to be an overnight task. One thing was certain: we were not going to show up at Ellen Bruce's door unless and until we had regained a measure of self-respect and a degree of confidence that we would not make a total mess of any relationship that might evolve.

But we had become painfully aware of a need for allies, for there to be somebody at least nominally on our side. Teddy, the iconoclast, if he still existed, could not possibly re-invent himself in austere isolation, taunting the world to like it, lump it, or go to hell. In his entire life, Teddy had never asked anyone for a favour; he took what he wanted, and if what he wanted was not forthcoming, he devised other ways to achieve his ends. Even if he had still had some former allies who might be approached, he had no common currency to offer in exchange. Moreover, the supporters he had once been able to call upon were not the sort of cohort who would take him where we needed to go.

But there remained in us a spark of audacity and the spiritual courage to apply it. If friends are of no use, or cannot be found, we must turn to our enemies—or former enemies. We decided to seek out Howard Silver. Here was an opportunity to practice a bit of humility, face up to our misdeeds, and set out on the long road to redemption. Howard had offered a thing of immense value, and being ill prepared, we had sent him away without an honourable response. Whether it would ever be possible to look him in the eye man to man or not, there was surely some unfinished business. We had to put matters right, if at all possible, before anything further could be accomplished toward the reclamation of Teddy and his misbegotten soul.

It wasn't difficult to track Howard down. We quickly learned that, despite all that had happened to him, there were still people who respected him and wished to count themselves his friends. (Lesson number one.) He lived in a modest flat above a store in a decidedly unfashionable neighbourhood. Our knock on his door elicited the sort of bark that could be associated only with a small, elderly, and somewhat asthmatic dog. It took a long minute for the door to open and we found ourselves facing the tired but placid gaze of a man who gave the impression that nothing would ever again surprise or disappoint him. The little dog continued to protest our unwelcome existence, in between wheezy breaths.

"You came to my door a while back and had the audacity to offer me something I could not possibly merit. I'm how having the audacity to face you and accept whatever you choose to do with me."

"Please come in. Don't be concerned about Senna. She's very old and a bit crotchety, but her bark is all that's left of her. She doesn't move very quickly, so you might have to step around her. May I offer you a cup of tea?"

"Thank you. I have no excuse for showing up here, except…"

"No excuse is required. By the way, I sort of expected you to come around at some point. I could see that you were greatly perturbed by my visit, and I know that your nature would not permit you to let the matter rest indefinitely."

Howard busied himself with tea preparation while holding a sotto voce monologue with the old dog, finally persuading her to accept our presence as normal and settle down in her bed in a corner beside an ancient TV set.

"Now that I'm here, I guess I have no idea what I really want to say to you, or what my purpose was in coming here at all. It just seemed to make some kind of sense, illogical as that may be. There's nothing I can actually offer you, no words that can be of any use."

"I'm pleased that you decided to come. It goes some way toward restoring my shaky faith in humanity."

"How is that?"

"Because it shows that you care. That you care about your own well-being. And it proves that my visit to you that day wasn't wasted. There remains hope for us, two aging and bedraggled men who used to think they were the smartest guys in the room, and have come to understand that in the end, it doesn't matter how smart we think we are. What matters is what we do with our lives."

Although this part of town was a bit more prosperous than ours, this apartment was probably even more Spartan than ours. It seemed that Howard's fortunes and Teddy's had intersected for a second time, once again each of them finding themselves at about the same level. Howard brought the tea to a somewhat wobbly table next to the tiny kitchen, obviously the spot where he was accustomed to taking his meals. We sat across from each other.

"Where should we begin? I suppose I should have asked you how you're feeling; you said before that you don't think you have long to live. I'm sorry if..."

"Never mind all that. We can't live forever—and why would you want to? Let's start by agreeing that neither of us owes the other a damn thing, other than common courtesy and respect for each other's opinions."

"I guess that works for me. But can you just drop everything that happened over the years, walk away and write it all off to... what? Experience?"

"Of course. What's done is done. There's no point in even discussing it any further. Why don't you tell me what you plan to do with what's left of your life—after all, you've probably still got a number of good years left in you."

At that point, neither of us had much of a notion of what we wanted to accomplish, or how to go about it. We only knew that we were determined to start over and salvage something out of whatever was left of Teddy McCoy. Over the next hour, we learned what happens to a man after everything he has, everything he is, has been lost.

When Howard Silver's business failed, he at first strove to salvage all he could of what had once been his fortune. He kept his family together, even though his home, which had been mortgaged in a futile attempt to keep the business going, was also lost. His son, who had been deeply engaged in the family business, realized there was no future there, so he left the company and took up a position with a firm in the Middle East. Two years later, he was killed there in an uprising. All this was too much for Howard's wife, who became a recluse, ending her days in a nursing home. Eventually she could no longer recognize her husband of forty years.

The fact that Howard Silver was able to rationalize all of this, retain his sanity, continue to live out his life, and not be hell-bent on exacting vengeance upon Teddy McCoy? Well, even to this day, I cannot begin to understand it all. Howard was in a permanent state of grieving; I suppose the act of grieving is what kept him functional.

For me, looking back on it now, the most astonishing aspect of all this is that the reclamation of Teddy McCoy became the project that helped Howard make sense of it all. He devoted his remaining time and energy to preventing Teddy from wasting what was left of his life, either in anger and resentment at his own downfall, or guilt and self-loathing at what he had done to Howard and to others. What we began to understand over the following few months, as we went through a long debriefing and emotional recovery together, was that survival has more to do with how one reacts than with the nature of the disaster itself.

Over those months, Howard became the closest and most influential friend we had ever had—in fact, probably the only true friend that Teddy McCoy ever gained during his life. Toward the end, as Howard's health continued to decline, our friendship deepened. Howard's resident soul and I began to establish an attachment, one of the very few such relationships I've ever been fortunate to experience. His soul, an entity I came to know as T'ai, helped me to understand a bit of what made Howard the extraordinary man that he was. T'ai was without question the most brilliant, noble, and inspiring soul that I have ever come to know. Howard was able to experience true peace of soul; were I to be an envious spirit, which I am not (some are, by the way!) I surely would have envied the relationship that Howard had with his spirit.

My attachment with T'ai was the most enriching experience I've ever had over many centuries and throughout the countless mortal lives I've accompanied. The best way I can describe being in close contact with T'ai would be that it was like sitting at the feet of a great teacher and mentor. T'ai opened up for me vistas of spiritual lives lived and mortal accomplishments that far exceeded any of my past experiences, or even my perceptions of what might be possible. Through T'ai, I learned the value of patience and forbearance, the ability to take the long view when beset with adversity. The realization of joy in the miracle of existence. The skills I inherited from T'ai will be with me always, to help me in dealing with a troubled host, even if I should encounter one as difficult as Teddy McCoy had proven to be.

Every soul is unique, endowed with a singular combination of skills, expertise, insight, drive, vision, and any number of other qualities that make it possible to propel its host along paths toward accomplishments that could only be reached by aligning with that soul and no other.

My entire experience with T'ai caused me, almost against my will, to speculate on how wonderful it might have been if I could have somehow reached an attachment with Ellen Bruce's resident soul. Surely hers was a truly remarkable spirit.

Best not to contemplate gifts that can never be granted.

****

The pursuit of wealth had lost all of its fascination for us. There was no chance that Teddy McCoy would ever be going back into the construction business. To continue living, of course, it was necessary for us to find ways of earning a living. To do so, we were first obliged to go through the unpleasant process of declaring personal bankruptcy.

Those who have not experienced that process are often resentful of those who have done so; after all, it's fundamentally unfair that a man should be able to simply walk away from his obligations, leaving those whose money he has borrowed (or, in some cases, swindled) with no compensation for their losses. Having experienced the process, we can attest that it is traumatic and deeply humiliating. No doubt there are some who take the bankruptcy route as a deliberate stratagem; in some cases, they manage by crafty legal manoeuvres to hide assets from legitimate creditors and emerge more or less whole, getting back into business in short order. Such men have no difficulty looking boldly into the faces of those people whose money they have taken and blown away. We certainly could not have done so.

The name of Teddy McCoy remained an object of public fascination long after the events of such notoriety and well after our business had collapsed. It was going to take a long time for that name to be relieved of its unsavoury reputation. Finding any sort of legitimate employment would be almost impossible.

There was, of course, the additional matter of two legs, one missing from above the knee and the other permanently deformed, making it difficult to get around. The prosthetic leg never really worked very well, largely because the remaining structure of the thigh it was attached to was compromised. But the highly visible results of that accident did provide an unforeseen opportunity to earn a modest living for a while.

Teddy's substantial knowledge of construction, and his personal experience with a major mishap (caused entirely by his insistence on proceeding with a risky endeavour in conditions that were far too dangerous) made Teddy McCoy an ideal person to advocate for safer practices in the building trades. The Safety Council paid for us to travel all over Ontario, delivering illustrated talks to contractors, their associations, insurers, and labour groups about unsafe practices and how to avoid them. It wasn't much, but it paid the rent and groceries.

We gave it our best effort, delivering extremely useful messages in language that our listeners could relate to, even though this was a role for which we were emotionally unsuited. Teddy would forever remain an outsider, a man whose experience and competence was unquestioned, but whose character and motives were often suspect. I don't believe that I, as Teddy's resident soul, was much help, apart from encouraging us to keep at it, be humble, and accept the skepticism of our audience as valid, given Teddy's notoriety.

We discovered that the one person we were entirely comfortable with was Howard. There was no need for pretense between us; everything that could have been said was past being necessary or useful. We began to spend long afternoons in his flat, over numerous cups of tea. Often, an hour would pass with hardly a word spoken. Our afternoons always ended as the light began to fail, because by then Howard would become a bit restless and we sensed that he wanted us gone, but was reluctant to signal that it was time for us to go. I wondered what it was that Howard had in mind. He surely had no place to be going in the evening and there was never any mention of visitors. Nevertheless, we understood that we ought to be on our way and took our leave, wandering back to our own silent little apartment.

And so we continued, until one bitterly cold day when Senna, well beyond her better days, was looking especially ill. The poor little mutt had remained in her bed by the TV the whole afternoon, hardly acknowledging our presence. As twilight began to descend and the icy wind picked up bits of snow left from the day before, hurling them against the windows, Howard seemed uneasy and rather than fidgeting as he usually did to signal the end of our afternoon, he put on a third pot of tea, and asked us if we had anything especially planned for the evening. Certainly, we did not.

"Do you think I could impose on you to stay for a while and keep an eye on Senna? There's nothing to be done with her, you understand. I just don't feel good about leaving her alone right now. It would only be for about three or four hours."

"Of course! I would be happy to stay. By all means, I'll keep the old girl company. I wasn't aware that you ever went out in the evenings. And especially on such a miserable night as this. None of my business, of course."

"Oh, I'm out for a while most evenings; especially on cold nights like this. That's when we're needed the most."

"What do you mean? Are you meeting someone?"

"Oh, yes. There are usually five or six of us making the rounds on a night like this. It's the homeless, you understand. So many of them can't face spending the night in the shelters where they would at least be warm. It's their demons that won't give them a moment of peace; life hasn't been kind to them and the close presence of other people, mostly strangers, is more than they can face. So they stay on the street. Hard for you and me to grasp, of course, but the cold, the wind, even the freezing drizzle—all of that they can deal with, but not being shut in where they can't control their own space. So we make our rounds, fetch them a blanket, a mug of coffee, a plastic tarp if it's raining. We can't change their lives, but we can at least reduce their misery for a few hours. It's not asking much of us to do that."

"I never knew. How long has this been going on?"

"Well, I suppose it's been going on for a very long time; but as for how long I've been involved, it seems to me that I've been at it more or less ever since my wife passed away, must be four or five years now. No organization, really, just a few volunteers. Blankets and such scrounged up by the local mission, a couple of coffee shops donating coffee, cookies; a couple of women from one of the downtown churches make sandwiches or soup. We meet at about six, collect our resources at the drop-in centre, the one that used to be a school, when people with homes and kids still lived down there; and then we hit the streets.

"By nine o'clock we've usually covered the territory and I'm almost always home before ten, unless we come across someone who needs serious medical attention, in which case we sometimes have to wait for an ambulance; and then there's the task of providing some unfortunate policewoman with whatever details we happen to know, which isn't much. You might not know this, but well over half of the cops who get stuck with that job are women. I suppose they're expected to be more empathetic, but that hasn't been my experience. It's not an assignment leading to quick promotion or high job satisfaction."

That was the first of several nights we spent with Howard's old mutt, who never seemed to get much better, just hung on. But her scrawny body eventually gave up the struggle and before the end of January, she breathed her last. Howard took the loss in stride, but his flat was even quieter and a good deal more forlorn than ever. There was then no further need for us to stay while Howard did his rounds; but we had nothing else of importance to be doing, so one night we suggested that we might tag along, despite the mobility challenges of Teddy's wrecked body. We were not likely to be much help, but we could at least keep Howard company, offer moral support.

And so that is how we became a familiar sight on the darkened streets, two aging and somewhat sickly looking men, poking into doorways, stairwells, bus shelters, under bridges; coaxing a bit of life into bodies much worse off than our own. It was an aspect of life in the city that we had known existed but had never come to grips with first hand. And a reality that to this day, I still find hard to really understand and impossible to accept.

Nothing remarkable took place the first night we accompanied Howard on his rounds. But on the second night, we were approaching a small figure huddled next to a bus shelter, when instantly we found ourselves thrust back more than twenty years, to the day Teddy first visited Ellen's studio. That sculpture that had so deeply unsettled the otherwise sanguine Teddy McCoy, depicting a ragged, homeless woman, was an exact image of the living person now lying here before us.

By what unimaginable process could Ellen have foreseen, and formed with her own hands, a precise image of the scene we would be facing here and now? What could it possibly mean? Could Ellen have had some strange kind of foreknowledge of the nightly endeavour that Teddy McCoy and his wayward spirit would be engaged in all these years later? Whether as spirit or mortal, I have no answers, but I do know that from that night onward, our mission took on an entirely greater meaning for us.

Night by night, we came to realize that the more brutal and unpleasant the weather was, and the more desperate the condition of our clients happened to be, the more satisfied we felt at the end of the evening. We understood that nothing was ever likely to change in the city environment, the shelter set-up, the welfare mechanisms, the prevalence of mental health, addiction, economic, or social issues—in short, all the factors that impacted homeless people. So everything that Howard, Teddy, and our little band of fellow volunteers were doing was always going to be a holding action, the proverbial little boy with his finger in the dyke; the ocean would not recede and new leaks would continue to appear.

In Teddy McCoy's former life, such a seemingly futile endeavour would have been unthinkable. For him, there had to be some hope of progress, some process of upward mobility; otherwise, why burden ourselves with a hopeless task? But we never came to feel that way, even on nights when everything was going wrong, when a homeless man or woman screamed insults at us for trying to help, when someone became deranged, confused, hostile; or worst of all, when a person we attempted to engage with refused to wake up and was never going to wake up again.

Walking those dark streets, we were accompanied on our patrols by a collection of men and women the likes of which we had never before known to exist. Drawn from every imaginable variation of humanity, our fellow volunteers covered pretty much the full spectrum of Toronto's immensely diverse population; a few were young, many quite old like ourselves. One could tell from their speech that, for most of them, their first learned languages had been something other than English.

We had been engaged in this enterprise for many weeks before we realized what it was that all of us had in common: every one of us was damaged in some manner—physically, emotionally, psychologically, spiritually, or whatever. I believe that it was our damaged state, the compelling fact of whatever trauma each had suffered, that drew us all together in this mission of mercy to our fellow man—an unspoken brotherhood of the wounded. Their origins, ancient or recent, might never be known. The only contact any of us had with each other was here, on our nightly patrol of the dark and desperate streets.

Were each of them, like the two of us, engaged in resetting the balance of their lives, living out the grief, errors, harm of their former lives? For most of them, as it was with us, performing this service to the dispossessed seemed to be fraught with difficulty, be it physical or emotional. More than once, at our brief assembly late at night at the drop-in centre, before dispersing for our separate homes, we encountered one or another of the group deeply distraught, struggling to regain their composure after a particularly harrowing rescue event.

I began to comprehend that there was something else going on here besides the business of keeping a scattered flock of derelicts alive for another night. There was another rescue mission in play here. We and our partners in this enterprise were engaged in resetting the balance in our own afflicted lives. For the paramedics, the police, the staff at the shelters, caring for those at risk was just a job. For us, it was something else entirely; it was a compulsion.

The makeup of the group was constantly changing. One or several new members would appear every few days while others fell away. A few seemed to vanish for a time, only to reappear some days or weeks later. It was the most unstructured enterprise imaginable. It never occurred to any of us to question where those absent for a time had been or why. Every person who showed up was welcomed; another willing pair of hands.

One of our group, a woman of indeterminate age, simply known as Mana, always had most of her face obscured by a scarf and a sort of veil; we assumed she must have been Muslim, but no one thought to ask about her habit of hiding her features. Until one windy night of driving rain when all of us were soaked through, shivering and utterly miserable long before the night's work was done, we straggled back to our meeting point in hopes of a reasonably hot cup of coffee and a chance to dry off a bit before dispersing to our homes. There, Mana removed her drenched coat, scarf, and veil. A glance at what was left of her shattered face left no doubt about the reason for the attire she had adopted.

Morris, a gigantic black man, appeared one night, asking if we needed a hand. His slight accent sounded vaguely Caribbean in origin; beyond that, we knew nothing about him. His manner was that of a person who had been abused in some manner and wished simply to be left alone in his suffering. Gentle, soft-spoken, he ended every sentence with a phrase such as "God willing," or "Praise the Lord," or sometimes simply "Amen."

One bitterly cold night on our rounds with Howard, we encountered a man huddled in a doorway, shrouded in a thin coat and a tattered tarpaulin. The wind had shifted, bringing the rain full force onto his useless refuge, and he was severely hypothermic, unable to move or speak. Howard went to find a phone to call for an ambulance. Covering the man would be of no use because he was already soaking wet; nothing we could do there would be able to revive him. There was no telling how long it would take for Howard to reach emergency contacts, or when an ambulance might finally arrive. Our patient might not survive until then.

Morris happened to be passing nearby, and seeing the situation, he simply picked the poor fellow up and carried him the six blocks to the nearest hospital. Each of us, regardless of our particular scars, brought our own unique talents to the task at hand.

Those nights on the grim streets of the city, we learned a great deal about the business of being human. And we learned a great deal about ourselves. Most of all, the man who had once been Teddy McCoy, along with his bedraggled spirit, began to understand why we had been placed on this earth, in this particular neighbourhood at this time. We came to know that we belonged here, that it was necessary and right that we, along with the rest of that wounded band of misfits, had found our way to this spot. Because there was work that we needed to do here.

Howard had just turned seventy-eight when we joined him on his self-imposed mission. It was unlikely that he would be able to continue much longer. By the time we were well into our second winter with him, we were becoming increasingly concerned that he was at risk of falling on the icy sidewalks and stairwells. Teddy's prosthetic didn't cope well with those conditions, either. It would have made more sense for each of us to be matched with a younger, fitter partner. But we had become accustomed to each other's pace, our limitations and moods.

Most tellingly, the miracle of the attachment that had been established between T'ai and myself more or less compelled us to remain together. Howard never suffered a serious fall, but there were numerous slips that resulted in cuts and bruises. His heart and lungs were weakening as the winter plodded on and his breathing during the bitterest nights became laboured. The days when he was simply unable to continue became more and more frequent. We tried making the rounds alone or with one or two of the other volunteers. Before spring, Howard's health had declined to the point where he was forced to stop making the rounds altogether.

For a month or so, we carried on alone, at least sporadically, usually paired up with someone as slow as we were, or at least an able-bodied person blessed with the patience to match our slow pace. We soon became another of those rescuers who appeared and then vanished periodically, without notice or explanation.

During the summer months, there were fewer of us, the need not being so great. As autumn came on, Howard's health had become so fragile that I felt compelled to spend most evenings with him at home. For both of us, our rescue mission was turning inward.

The only relative who ever took an interest in Howard was an officious, impatient niece named Phyllis, who put in an appearance every few months. She usually badgered him for a day or two about moving into a nursing home and attempted to reorganize his diet; then, having had her say, she would disappear. She lived in the extreme outer suburbs on the western fringe of the city and continually complained about the difficulty of driving "practically to the end of the world" to visit him. She saw Teddy as a bad influence and a general nuisance, even worse than "that smelly little dog" had been. Howard bore her abuse stoically, but was always relieved when she left.

In addition to his endearing personality and unconditional friendship, one of the legacies that Howard bequeathed to us was an appreciation for cool, mellow jazz. Several times during that spring and summer, we somehow found the money to spend an evening in one of the local clubs if one of his favourite groups was performing.

But in general, nightclubs were well outside of Howard's limited budget or ours. His collection of CDs was small, but its superb quality came through even when played on his disgraceful old portable player, an artifact that had probably served some teenager as a boom box earlier in its beaten-up life. Howard made us promise to make off with the CDs as soon as he died and make sure Phyllis didn't get her hands on them. He needn't have worried about that; Phyllis couldn't have cared less about his music—or anything else of his, given the obvious lack of any financial inheritance to be had.

Howard owned nothing else of value. The combined contents of his flat and ours would not have drawn the interest of a flea market operator. He did his modest shopping at a small neighbourhood grocery, and having once given up his nightly volunteer work, he rarely travelled more than a dozen blocks from home. He called on the services of a taxi for his monthly visits to his doctor to deal with a lingering lung inflammation, a malady that I was convinced had originated on his mid-winter nights prowling the downtown streets, ministering to the needs of the homeless.

We fell into the habit of accompanying him on those medical visits, I suppose, hoping to gain insight into his condition, or to reassure us that he would still be with us for a while. Nothing the doctor said in our presence was the least bit enlightening, simply that Howard needed to stay on his medication and avoid stress.

We were in a taxi, about halfway home from such a visit on an afternoon in October, one of those glorious, sun-drenched autumn days that are the best time of year in our part of the world, when Howard suddenly stopped speaking in mid-sentence and collapsed. We frantically rerouted the cab to the nearest hospital while we did what we could to revive him. On our arrival at the emergency entrance, Howard was hurriedly wheeled away, leaving Teddy standing there, in his mind, hoping that Howard could be saved.

But my own attachment with T'ai left no room for uncertainty; Howard's body and his resident soul had parted company.

I had never before in all my sojourns with mortals felt so alone and bereft.

Finding the Way Home

HOWARD AND HIS MAGNIFICENT SOUL had given us a new lease on life by reinstating normalcy, purpose, and, above all, understanding. And yet, as transformative as Howard's forgiveness had been for us, it in no way relieved the harshness of our own judgment of our behaviour and our life's accomplishments. With Howard gone, the wonderful attachment of our spirits was also lost. Despite having reached a state of rapport between mind and soul, despite now being able to influence Teddy's state of mind in a very much more direct manner than ever before, I yet found our situation deeply troubling. Teddy McCoy was not at peace. I understood that this state of discontent was brought about by a lack of atonement. Redemption is not a simple, painless process.

There are a number of very different kinds of funeral: the pompous, phony parade staged for the departure of some illustrious dignitary or politician, accompanied by glowingly insincere accolades; the celebratory farewell, brightened by personal reminiscences and jokes shared by loved ones finding themselves laughing through their tears; and the heartbroken, unalloyed ordeal of grief at the untimely loss of a beloved son, soulmate, sister, or whatever.

And then there's the worst kind of funeral of all: the one where almost no one seems to have been interested enough to show up, and those who do appear seem to regret having done so, and only wish to get the damn thing over with. At such a funeral, it seems appropriate that there should be foul weather. The weather gods, if such there be, had clearly got the message for Howard's last day above ground. The fine weather that had graced Howard's last day of life was only a sad memory; the icy drizzle of November had arrived several weeks ahead of schedule.

The funeral director was obliged to assign several of his own staff to do the honours, since potential pallbearers who had been associated in any way with Howard's family and friends were almost impossible to find. For us, the most distressing part of the whole miserable affair was that we were prevented from lending a hand; when the funeral director found that of the three men who stepped forward to carry the coffin, one was a man named McCoy with a badly fitted artificial leg, we were told politely but firmly that our services were not required. That decision was ably reinforced by Howard's spiteful niece, who made it chillingly evident that we were unwelcome at the affair.

As we stood shivering in our raincoats or huddled under umbrellas at the graveside, about a dozen or so strangers, hoping that the minister would make his final prayers as brief as possible, we found ourselves face to face with an equally glum but startlingly familiar figure, that of Ellen Bruce.

How had she become aware of Howard's passing, a man she was unlikely to have known? It could only have come about because she had been unobtrusively keeping watch over us. What a tragic vigil that must have been for her, knowing that Teddy had—and let's face it, with help from me—destroyed everything that could have developed between us. I cannot clearly recall the conflicting and confused thoughts that passed through us during those brief moments before and immediately after the last "Amen."

As the small group broke up and scattered quickly, the two of us, a hobbling, shivering, and deeply disturbed Teddy McCoy and a taciturn Ellen Bruce, were left standing there in the drizzle, neither able to find words. What possible words could there be at such a time?

After a minute or two had passed, with still nothing having been said, Ellen linked her arm with Teddy's and we silently made our way out of the cemetery and to the last waiting taxi by the entrance. Ellen gave an address and shortly we were seated in a quiet bar a few blocks from our apartment. We had long since given up any sort of alcoholic beverage, Teddy's one remaining kidney in its weakened state having made its limitations clear in a most uncompromising fashion. But under the circumstances, and finding this body of ours in a thoroughly chilled state, we agreed to a shot of brandy.

After what was probably the better part of an hour, but somehow seemed to pass in an instant, Ellen appeared to be satisfied that Teddy was in a condition that would enable him to walk the four blocks to his home. She took his arm again, and we made our way through the darkening streets. Our inclination toward conversation, having been limited while we were in the bar, was even more subdued with wind-driven drizzle in our faces. At our door, we finally found the presence of mind to thank Ellen and invite her in, but she refused.

"This is not a good time, Teddy. Who knows if there will ever be a good time for us, but in any case, this is not it. Just promise me one thing: that you will phone me in a few days. As soon as you feel a bit more like yourself. I cannot bring myself to just say goodbye and walk away this time. Would you do that for me? Just call me one day and say hello? I'm not expecting anything, just the chance to hear your voice and to know somehow that you're OK."

"Ellen, surely you must know that I'm a lost cause."

"I know. Call me anyway."

"Alright, if that's what you want. I'll call, but it may take me a while to get around to it."

"I know. That's just the way it is with us. Goodnight, Teddy McCoy."

And that was it. As soon as we were alone in the apartment, what was left of Teddy's physical and emotional composure crumbled. I found myself bound to a still fully dressed and quite-damp body sprawled across the bed, shivering uncontrollably and attempting not to weep. After some time, Teddy drifted off to sleep, and rather than any clumsy effort at directing our dreams, a task that I had fumbled so badly on a number of occasions, I took my own troubled repose. There would be plenty of time in the coming days to figure out what, if anything, to do about Ellen.

What I, being a mere spirit, had not taken fully into account was the physical frailty of my host's body. The emotional impact of the loss of our only friend, combined with a weakened immune system and a single damaged kidney, had taken its toll on what was left of a once-robust Teddy McCoy. He arose from bed at some point in the early morning hours only to disrobe and don pyjamas before collapsing in bed once more.

After another full day had passed with little or no movement, I began to be much more concerned and tried to recapture Teddy's conscious attention, convince him that he needed to take action to keep himself alive; take a warm bath; eat something. Better still, call a doctor. Spirits find it hard to relate to the specifics of the host body's mechanisms and state of health; we know if there's a fever by how the body behaves, but we cannot really tell if it's serious or not. The closeness I had been able to achieve with Teddy emotionally and psychically did not enable me to bridge the physical gap between body and spirit. Simply put, a spirit has virtually no physical awareness or insight; the physical realm remains beyond our grasp no matter how intimate we become in spirit.

I believe that the only thing that kept Teddy and me from arriving at our final parting during those days was a haphazard aspect of Teddy's personality: his compulsive need to know what was going on in the world around him, despite having left the public sphere. And despite knowing that he was never going to become an active businessman again. For that reason, Teddy still subscribed to a daily newspaper, and it was that which saved him.

After six or seven papers had piled up at our door, it occurred to someone, I've no way of knowing who, to begin asking questions. A neighbour knocked, received no answer, and apparently contacted our landlord. His economic self-interest prompted him to find out if his lone tenant was still alive (after all, owning an apartment that has recently played host to a dead body for some time is troublesome, and bad for business). When he retrieved his key and opened the door, he discovered a decidedly unwell tenant, semi-conscious and unresponsive to the simplest of questions.

A half-hour later, we were in hospital, and there we stayed for the better part of a week while efforts were made to overcome dehydration, stabilize body temperature, and induce Teddy to eat. I spent all of my efforts during that time attempting to recapture Teddy's conscious mind, his awareness of the presence (and I like to think, the importance) of his resident immortal soul. All this with the objective of convincing him that life was actually worth living and that there still remained for him an opportunity to do something meaningful with his life. Life is precious; it should not be wasted. I had already invested a good deal of effort in this fellow. In spite of compelling evidence, I was convinced that he had potential and merit. I was in no way prepared to give up on him yet.

But I was also conflicted, because even though I was doing my best to strengthen my host's state of mind and encourage him to grab hold of life, I was reluctant to prompt him to call Ellen as he had agreed to do. I couldn't determine whether any relationship with her would be a good thing for either of them. Or if such an outcome was even possible. The emotional obstacles in Teddy's path were enormous. And I was unable to fully understand

Ellen's state of mind. My initial meddling in their affair had gone very badly. I decided to wait and see what would transpire, and I certainly wanted to be on solid ground before I made any further attempts to influence things. For the time being, my first priority was helping Teddy to become a great deal more at peace with himself.

I cannot say whether my influence helped very much, but over the next couple of weeks, Teddy's natural strength of character, or perhaps his sheer stubbornness, pulled him through. He fought off the illness, began to eat regular meals, albeit skimpy ones, and in due course, he was sent home to recuperate. The immediate problem I foresaw was the sheer emptiness of not just that dingy apartment, but the hollowness of Teddy McCoy's entire life. As the gloom of November crept by and a wintery December arrived, the fact that everyone around us was planning for Christmas heightened our awareness of our isolated and directionless existence.

Teddy purposely forced himself to go out for a few minutes almost every day, to the local grocery store or to a cheap lunch counter now and then for a better meal than whatever he might throw together for himself at home. But there was no real motivation in all of this; we were simply going through the motions, pretending to be alive, and I feared his determination to survive would not last unless something were to bring about a change in routine, create a point of focus. The lack of a purpose in life, having nothing to do, nothing to hope for and, worst of all, nothing and no one to love can be a death sentence, more overwhelming than the worst diseases. I began to fear that punishing himself for his failings might become Teddy's only conscious occupation.

As I suppose I mentioned before, the affairs of humans seldom seem to run in predictable or straight lines. Having little to occupy his mind and being physically inactive due to his weakness and mobility limitations, Teddy slept poorly. When he did drift off, he seldom achieved a deep, solid sleep state, and it took very little to disturb him. Small sounds in the building—neighbours' doors slamming, children's voices on the stairs or in the street, sirens in the night—all interrupted his sleep. And a new source of annoyance had arrived on the scene: over several nights at odd hours, a dog began barking, the sound apparently coming from an alleyway behind the building.

For some annoying reason, the beast chose to bark directly opposite our bathroom window, a window that we always left open just a bit for much-needed ventilation. When one or another of the neighbours shouted at the dog, it would stop barking, but a few minutes later it would begin to whine, which was every bit as effective in keeping Teddy awake.

Finally, in frustration, we got out of bed, dressed, and went downstairs and out to put a stop to the noise. Our intention was to discover whose dog this was and confront the owner. An initial search of the alleyway failed to turn up any dog at all. Perhaps someone had finally dealt with the matter, or the dog had just wandered off. But as soon as we re-entered the building, there was that annoying whine again. And this time it was right there, outside the utility door, next to the garbage chute. The area was quite dark, so we returned to the apartment to retrieve a flashlight, determined now to settle the matter.

With the light, it took only a moment to spot the animal crouching beside the door, shivering and whimpering. It was a pathetic specimen of indeterminate breed, its hair matted and filthy, undoubtedly infested with fleas. No collar. Clearly a stray, and one that had been on the go for quite some time. The creature appeared to be simultaneously frightened and yet desperate for human contact. It was 4 a.m. on a Saturday, no chance of raising anyone at Animal Control. Even the Humane Society would not likely be reachable before Monday. What to do?

No matter how badly life had beaten him down, Teddy McCoy never ceased being a resourceful man. Back upstairs to obtain an old canvas belt that had seen better days, out of which Teddy improvised a collar. There was no way we were taking this dog into the apartment, fleas not being welcome guests. Fortunately, we had access to the storage locker room in the basement. Depositing the dog in there and locking the door again, we went upstairs to get a dish for water, an old smock that would do for a blanket, and a handful of leftover chicken. The dog swallowed the chicken in two gulps, lapped a bit of water, and then rolled over on his back, tail thrashing, begging for attention, any gesture of kindness.

We found the creature enormously appealing, but at the same time utterly disgusting in its current state. The next challenge would certainly be getting it to lie down and keep quiet until it could be dealt with properly. Getting the dog to settle down on the smock took the better part of an hour and a lot more patience than Teddy McCoy was known for. Every time we left the locker room and closed the door, the whining would start up again. But on the sixth attempt, when we closed the door, all was quiet.

As expected, we were unable to reach anyone at the City or the Humane Society Saturday or Sunday. Conversing with answering machines, navigating phone trees can try anyone's patience, and Teddy had little to spare. However, pet supply stores were open, so flea powder and dog food were not a problem. Fortunately, ours being one of those old-style apartment buildings left over from the 1950s, there was a shared laundry room in the basement, and that included a pair of big old-style concrete laundry tubs, perfectly adequate for bathing a dog.

Following a thorough bath and the determined use of a pair of scissors, we ended up with a very clumsily clipped but reasonably clean dog. With the smock washed and dried, the area sprayed, and the dog dusted again, there was hope that the vermin were under control, at least for the time being. After a generous meal and a short walk in the alley to relieve himself, the dog seemed content to settle down on the makeshift bed in the locker room.

He was still visibly exhausted from his ordeal on the streets. Come Monday, there should be no problem passing this stray to the Humane Society to deal with. A good deed well done, and no more disturbed sleep. Our thrice-daily visits to the dog were greeted with enthusiasm and…

Well, you can see where all this is leading. On Monday morning, we decided it would be best to make sure the dog was properly fed and given a decent walk before attempting to get someone to come and pick him up. We could not possibly take the dog anywhere on the bus and it might be some time before anyone arrived to take him away. When Teddy spoke to the Humane Society on the phone, they were adamant that they had no ability to collect animals; they had to be delivered to their facility. When we phoned the city again, we were placed on hold, and listened to a succession of musical interludes, while being assured every few minutes that our call was important to them.

The outcome was predictable. By the end of the day on Monday, Teddy's initial determination to get Animal Control to do their duty had morphed into a determination to say "to hell with their stupid bureaucracy" and take action himself. The dog got a second bath on Tuesday, a fresh flea treatment, and a somewhat better clipping (although still far from looking well groomed). This nondescript little mongrel had lucked out and found a home.

Even at the beginning, in its most disgusting condition, there had been something about the animal that had appealed to Teddy. It was only a week later that we realized the connection: the dog reminded us of Howard's little old mutt, Senna—not in appearance but in its mannerisms. In acquiring this dog, we had regained a piece of our relationship with Howard. That was how this dog acquired the peculiar name O'Senna. Later, when anyone inquired about that nonsensical name, and noted that there didn't appear to be anything about the dog that was the least bit Irish, Teddy just grinned and insisted that the dog's name was a mystery. As far as

I recall, he never explained the name to anyone, regarding it as a private joke between him and his memories of our best friend.

A daily routine was soon established, beginning with a short walk the length of the back alley, down to the first corner. That was where Mrs. Patterson's brindle cat would be lying in wait to hiss at O'Senna, who pretended not to be aware of the cat's presence, even though anyone the least bit familiar with O'Senna's moods could see that he was gritting his teeth in annoyance.

Our progress from that point onward became more leisurely, inspecting a strip of overgrown grass (mostly weeds, really) bordering what used to be a schoolyard that had been given a new life as a parking lot. It was a miserable patch of greenery in a neighbourhood that otherwise consisted of pavement, most of it badly cracked and heaved, or haphazardly patched. That litter-strewn patch of weeds was the only piece of ground that bore any vague resemblance to the natural world, and it suited O'Senna as a spot to do his business. It was notable that O'Senna turned out to be the only creature, human or otherwise, who had ever been able to regulate Teddy McCoy's daily timetable and itinerary.

Over the years, my connection with Teddy led me to the notion that a good deal of the essence of a mortal life consists of trying, consciously or otherwise, to find one's way home. That wayward little dog had, despite all its misfortunes, succeeded in finding its way home. But for Teddy, that had proven impossible. From the beginning, he belonged nowhere. As a boy, he had been at best an aggravating youngster who had to be tolerated, at worst a serious menace who had somehow to be managed. He belonged nowhere and held allegiance to no one but himself. Throughout his tempestuous career, that had never changed. Would Teddy McCoy ever find his way home?

****

With no prompting from me, Teddy finally did call Ellen and went to face her. Not with hope for any sort of reconciliation; her forgiveness was in fact a hindrance, because he had done nothing to earn it. Instead, he was driven by a determination to demonstrate, largely to himself, that he had the courage to face up to his own failings, acknowledge his mistakes, and accept whatever retribution might await him. I believe that in his mind, seeing Ellen again face to face was a form of self-flagellation, a way of coming to terms with the fact that nothing he could ever do would set matters right.

Ellen still lived in the flat above what had been her studio, now little more than a warehouse of abandoned projects, half-finished pieces, rejected submissions to this or that gallery or sponsor, clay models that may or may not have found their way to a foundry at some point. She poked around the place most days, half-heartedly working up ideas that no one took any interest in. It had been several years since anything she made had been sold, the works of her heydays largely forgotten.

She had been approached by an animated film studio to teach clay modelling three afternoons a week to a new generation of animators, who were turning their backs on computer-generated animation, and were searching for the realism of solid figures. To her surprise, she had found it stimulating to spend time with that circle of young people—kids, really—who regarded her as a cross between a historical artifact and a path to a future state of their own imagining. The job paid very little, but Ellen had learned to live on not very much. Even not very much hope.

Teddy arrived at the old studio empty handed, deliberately so. He wanted to make it clear that he was not offering anything because nothing he could possibly have offered would be sufficient. Ellen brewed up tea, and they settled into a couple of battered old chairs in a corner of the studio. Teddy insisted that he would not stay long, he was just fulfilling a promise; and he would not go upstairs to her flat.

"I may go there someday, but only when I belong there. At present, I don't."

"Where do you belong, Teddy?"

"I have no idea. I've been thinking about that a lot. I used to scoff at that sort of question. I figured that a man decides for himself where it is that he belongs. He makes his own space, occupies it in his own way; tells the world where to get off."

"And what do you believe now?"

"I believe that I've spent most of my life kidding myself. I don't have any answers. I'm not even sure I know how to ask the right questions. Maybe you've got things figured out, I sure haven't."

"It seems to me that the world has more or less had its fill of both of us; we're a pair of left-overs. You used to fret about us not having anything much in common, apart from both being outsiders in our own way. Guess what? Nothing much has changed. Except that we no longer delude ourselves into thinking that we have something unique to offer the world, to make it sit up and take notice."

"I guess you're right."

"And you know, that isn't necessarily a bad thing. Maybe we can agree on that. Anyway, drink up your tea if you still want it. I'm not offering you anything to eat. First, because you refuse to come upstairs to eat, and second, because I'm actually the world's second-worst cook. I can't even stand to eat what I cook, so I don't bother; I eat sandwiches and junk food, the way it comes out of a bag. So how about us going down to the deli? It's only a couple of blocks and you seem to be getting around well enough for that."

****

Over the next few weeks, Teddy and Ellen often had dinner together at various eateries, their selection based on affordability, relative quiet, and accessibility; and reachable without a costly taxi fare. One of those afternoons at Ellen's studio, as we were idly sipping tea and talking about not very much, her phone rang. We sensed an uncharacteristic unease in Ellen during her brief conversation; and after it ended, she chose to comment on it, even though it was, of course, none of our business. "One of my young… students; Perdita—my little lost one. I still like to kid myself that I have something worthwhile to pass on. But I wasn't cut out to be a teacher; too much of a loner."

"So, who is she?"

"Just a dreamer, something like what I once was, I suppose. I'm probably doing this young woman's talent more harm than good, infecting her mind with my outmoded ideas about art. I still cling to this outrageous nonsense about sculpture having something to do with beauty. Our lessons, if that's what they are, happen whenever she has the time and I have the inclination. She's working two part-time jobs besides her studies at the OCA. When she gets fed up with the industrial drivel they throw at students nowadays and finds herself with a bit of time between shifts, she comes to me. She'll be here in half an hour. You… might find it… interesting to meet her."

There was something left unsaid, buried between Ellen's words, that suggested it would be better to for us leave. Of course, the last thing any teacher needs is an observer hanging about, with nothing to do except get in the way. Ellen shrugged off our concern, insisting that there was no reason to avoid her students; but from that day on, we thought it would be prudent to phone before dropping by unannounced at the old studio. All we ever learned about Ellen's students was that while there had been several from time to time, now there was only the one. As Ellen put it, Perdita at twenty-six was a "late bloomer"—almost the same age that Ellen had been when we had first met. That was about all we learned about Perdita. She remained for us a somewhat tantalizing enigma, and we didn't get to meet her. And yet, her name, suggestive of something lost, was impossible to forget.

Every few days, Ellen would stop by our apartment in the early afternoon, the time of day when we would take our main walk of the day with O'Senna, past the corner, to where Mrs. Patterson's cat awaited. Walking with a dog relieves humans of any need for explanation about awkward matters or unresolved issues that we don't wish to discuss. The dog's agenda is simple and straightforward enough, and if someone else wishes to tag along, there's no need to explain that, either. We were just two people with a dog, nothing more complicated than that.

I interfered in this process as little as possible, leaving these two mortals to find their way by themselves. They had quietly become comfortable with each other, but Teddy, within his own troubled psyche, was nowhere close to a meaningful atonement. Whenever he stopped by the old studio, his hands remained empty. He did not go upstairs. He had still not found his way home.

But we did have something that Teddy could share with Ellen, something of immense value to us, something that had been bequeathed to us by our dearest friend: a love for and appreciation of cool, gentle jazz. When Teddy decided to offer this gift to Ellen, he was at first hesitant, fearing that it would not appeal to her. Several times he was on the point of suggesting to her a late-night visit to our favourite jazz cellar, the one that Howard had introduced us to. Repeatedly, Teddy changed his mind at the last minute, and we just had dinner at one of the usual spots and went back to our separate homes.

But it finally occurred to us that we were hesitating because we feared rejection. And that made up Teddy's mind for him, with no interference from me. Ellen never accused him of any wrongdoing, had long ago forgiven him unconditionally. And that, for Teddy, was an unresolved problem. Her rejection, her condemnation, was exactly what he felt he needed, what he deserved. He made up his mind to ask Ellen to accompany him to his favourite night spot, reveal to her his love of the music, and urge her to share this love with him. Whether she accepted or refused, either outcome would be good. I again emphasize that I had no part in this decision, did my best not to influence Teddy. But when that decision was made, I knew that it was the right one. Sometimes, the most helpful thing a soul can do is just to stay out of the way.

Although Ellen happily accepted the invitation, we couldn't determine right away whether she was looking forward to this outing or just willing to accommodate one of Teddy's whims. We soon discovered the truth: simply that Ellen had very seldom been exposed to such music, knew practically nothing about it, and went along with us to the club with an open mind. But once settled at a tiny round table at the club, wrapped in the velvety closeness of a muted trombone and the soft cadence of a string bass, she soon began to understand the extent of Teddy's devotion to this music, its emotional significance in his life, its relevance to the memory of our best friend. This was an aspect of Teddy that she had never anticipated. The music soon took root in Ellen's artistic awareness, captured her imagination, and swept her away. By the end of the evening, she was hooked.

Because there was a cover charge (and because Teddy tipped more generously than our budget could really afford) the barman let us get away with nursing just two drinks each over the whole evening. For us, time had vanished, and we never moved until the musicians had finished their last set and were packing up their instruments. As Teddy was helping Ellen into her coat at the door, with no anticipation or conscious thought, she turned into his arms and they glided into a kiss. A kiss that went on and on, a kiss that neither ever wanted to end, a kiss that had been lost and forgotten for twenty-five years and that had finally found its way home.

We made our silent way up the steps, with no awareness of where we were or how we had got to street level. And no plans as to where we were going next. It was well past midnight, the street practically deserted. Lost in the mood of the evening, the music, and each other, it had not occurred to us to phone for a cab while we were still inside the club. We had been the last patrons to leave, and by now the place was locked up for the night. Our only option was to walk down to Gerard Street in hopes that there would still be an occasional streetcar running. There might well be an hour wait for a streetcar, but that didn't matter. We were in no hurry. Gerard Street was only three blocks down.

Rather than walking an extra four blocks back to Yonge Street before heading south, we took a small side street lined with down-at-the-heels rooming houses, their minuscule front yards a tangle of dumpsters, trash, and illegally parked cars. The street was very dark, and this was a pretty rough part of town, but then it was only three blocks, a short walk even for us. Arm in arm we strolled, exhilarated in each other's company, our rediscovery of each other. We were entirely oblivious to the chill of the January night. And to the presence of a dark figure emerging from the gloom of an alcove.

A powerful hand grasped Ellen's free arm and wrenched her away from Teddy. Left suddenly off balance from having had Ellen jerked away from our left arm, we stumbled and wavered, that one damaged leg and shaky prosthetic struggling to keep us from falling. All we could see, all we could focus on, was the glint of a handgun pressed to Ellen's head.

"Hand over your wallet and make it quick! I got no time to piss around! One bad move and the lady gets it!" The guy was extremely agitated, gasping, the hand holding the gun shaking violently, barely able to keep it against Ellen's head. This was a man badly strung out on something.

Teddy was momentarily frozen by the terror in Ellen's eyes, unable to react. His hesitation was deadly; the assailant lifted the gun and brought it down hard against Ellen's head. She grunted and would have fallen if the guy had not been holding on to her with his free hand. Ellen was stunned, her eyes blank, confused. Teddy didn't think. There was no time. He just reacted, the old Teddy McCoy who backed down from no one.

He lunged forward, grabbed the hand holding the gun. There was a roar of rage from the man as he and Teddy crashed into each other and Ellen fell to the sidewalk. A single bang exploded in Teddy's ear and a moment later Ellen was just conscious enough to hear footsteps, someone running away at top speed. Both Ellen and Teddy were lying on the sidewalk, Ellen struggling to reach out to Teddy and trying to clear her head, make sense of what had happened.

"It's OK, Teddy. The guy gave up and took off. We'll be OK."

"Teddy!… Oh my God, Teddy!!"

I had been released. Teddy McCoy had found his way home.

Continuance

DURING THIS LIFE, TEDDY MCCOY, you have become another part of me. What we have experienced together will live on. My next host will not be consciously aware of all that, but it will be there, in the background, beyond consciousness. Your own unique spirit, the essence that you were born with and that made you *you* will prevail, one more new thin layer, a flavour, a catch of tuneless melody suspended just beyond hearing, as I continue my journey through eternity.

No, we will not "meet again" because you and I will never really part. You will remain a part of me, and we will face the next host together. Each new person has a spark of immortality; it illuminates the resident soul, for good or ill, and carries onward, ever onward...

The ephemeral nature of human existence can rob it of meaning. If nothing that a person does during his life affects even the smallest aspect of the ongoing human story, he is likely to be soon totally forgotten. Leaving no footprints, how can it be said that his life had meaning? Yes, while living, he matters to someone, if only to himself, but that is only a transitory condition. Even the great and powerful will eventually have their record become blurred, faded, even perhaps distorted, depending on who it is that wins the wars or the elections, who writes the histories.

But every host that I have accompanied has left a mark on me, never to be lost, amended, or forgotten, and is thereby made immortal. Those experiences, those insights, even the bitter scars of loss, can at any time be brought to the fore to offer comfort, wisdom, courage, inspiration, to any number of future hosts. Therein surely lies meaning.

****

I take little interest in the day-to-day activities of mankind in general. Dealing with one badly behaved human at a time keeps me fully occupied. Nevertheless, I did happen to notice a fairly unobtrusive bronze sculpture that has just now been placed in a small neighbourhood park, a relatively low-income part of town that one would seldom expect to have been chosen as the site for such a piece of public art. Life-size, it appears to depict a man with an awkward stance, as if his legs are damaged in some way. There is no inscription to inform the casual observer who this man might be, why the work was placed here, or who the sculptor was. A more careful scrutiny of the work will, however, reveal the unmistakable evidence of a loving hand in its creation.

The man is accompanied by a scruffy, nondescript little dog. He appears to be an ordinary sort of man, even poorly dressed; a man of no consequence. But the significance of this work lies in the physical attitude of the figure, the tilt of his head, the gaze of his eye: it is unquestionably an attitude of defiance.

****

So that is my story. The time approaches when I must leave you, as well. Teddy is no more, and now I must move on; a new engagement awaits.

Before leaving you, I want to make it understood that I claim no credit for Teddy McCoy's reclamation—if that's what took place here. In my own clumsy fashion, I pointed him toward what

I perceived as better choices, and undertook to smooth over some of the ragged edges that unnecessarily complicated his life. But for my influence to have any effect whatsoever, he had to be prepared, and it was the combined impact of Ellen's selfless love, and the presence of T'ai, Howard's magnificent soul, that touched Teddy, opened up his mind, and made it possible for him to achieve a measure of inner peace.

****

With my troubled journey with Teddy McCoy having come to an end, I'm ready to begin the process all over again: select a new host from the choices offered, and find my way into the emerging consciousness of an infant, and then a growing child. Once again, I'll be bound up within the strictures of human mortality. There's nothing else for me to be doing. Best get on with fulfilling my destiny, whatever that might be.

But for some reason unknown to me, there seems to be a pause in proceedings. It's this hiatus, this unexplained opening, that has enabled me to tell my story until now. But surely I'm done with all that now; it's time to move on.

And yet, I'm not being offered any prospective hosts. I'm drifting, at a loss, truly on my own. In such a state of unaccustomed idleness, I feel once again the loss of my *attachment* with T'ai as sharply as the day that T'ai and Howard's body parted company. Nor is there any human mortal connection for me, and that's a state of normalcy that I'm missing. Never mind how frustrating it can be for the soul. When set loose—between jobs, as it were—a soul more or less wanders; it is nowhere and everywhere at once, disconnected from place, time, and physical existence.

I'm not at all sure that my successive engagements have even taken place in sequence of time, as you humans would perceive it. The physicists don't even seem to have made up their mind about what time really is, how it works. Can it cycle backwards? Scary thought! I have no idea. All I know is that I should be moving along onto my next assignment. My current state here, awaiting reincarnation, is similar to what you may have experienced when sitting in one of those deliberately uncomfortable plastic chairs in some anteroom, waiting for your name to be called. There seems to be nothing I can do but wait.

So I drift…

****

I'm experiencing something entirely new to me. I'm aware of what is going on in various parts of the world; not as if I'm physically "floating" and observing from above, as you might imagine. It's more as if I am suspended in a space that doesn't exist physically, watching events without actually seeing them. I have no words to describe it, but for want of a better explanation, I can only suggest to you a hologram that is invisible and yet very real to me.

There's a place here I seem to know, but I can't make out just what or where it is. Some people I think I've known arrive; depart. Then there's another place, one that I certainly don't know; eventually, I understand that it's an apartment; a tiny hole of a place, probably a flat above a store in the poorer part of some city. I become aware of a young woman who seems to live here. I gradually begin to believe that I ought to know her; but I do not. It's all terribly unclear: why I'm observing all this, wondering who this young woman is, where it's taking place—and above all, why it concerns me, and what I'm supposed to do about it.

Time seems to pass: Is it days? Hours? Years? I cannot tell. But no, it can't be years. The woman doesn't seem to age. And yet she changes in some manner that isn't clear to me. She seems troubled, unsure of where life is leading her, confused. But of course, that's a normal state of affairs. You mortals spend your entire lives in a state of confusion; I suppose it's because you never get to practice before embarking on a life. There's no training program, no book of instructions, no stage manager in the wings. Your life is a beta version, full of bugs that no programmer ever gets around to fixing. You have no option but to just stumble through it, crashing into hard objects, plunging into pools of heartbreak that you didn't know existed.

For a while, I perceive the apartment without really "seeing" it, and then I'm gone; somewhere else—or nowhere at all, who knows? But I keep coming back, and every time I do, the woman, who I now understand is in her late twenties, is even more troubled than she was before. And she is moving more slowly. Laboured, as if she suffers from some illness or disability. And yet she seems to be young and healthy. She's deeply worried about something. I feel her anxiety more distinctly than I can assess her physical condition. That's the way it is with a soul: the physical realities of the body are hard for us to grasp, but it's easy for me to judge a mortal's state of mind, even if I cannot connect with their resident spirit. It dawns on me that what I somehow ought to recognize is this young woman's spirit, its significance to me. But I do not.

It's all due to my shortcomings, the soul's inability to understand the material world, in general, and the realities of the human body, in particular; that's why it has taken me so many observations to finally realize what it is that's troubling the woman physically, making her seem uncomfortable; and that it's probably the same thing that is the cause of her anxiety. She's pregnant; and not enjoying the experience. Which perhaps means that she's unmarried, facing parenthood on her own.

Unbidden, recollections of Janet McCoy are crowding back to me, that period of weeks—or months, I suppose—while I had been waiting for that embryo to launch itself (and me) on the helter-skelter life that even now continues to haunt me. The rueful knowledge of my failure to measure up! Am I doomed to go through this whole frustrating odyssey all over again, domiciled with another misbegotten bastard kid, fighting the world all its life?! Have I stumbled so badly with Teddy McCoy that I've been assigned to "repeat the grade" like a lazy good-for-nothing school kid? Is that what this is all about?

But no, this is a very different woman; she bears no earthly resemblance to Janet McCoy. She's sober, self-possessed, seems to be intelligent. There are no skanky party animals hanging about. In fact, I've yet to detect a visitor of any kind to the apartment. If this lady has a problem with friends, it seems to be the lack thereof. I still have no idea why I'm being shown this woman, but I'm beginning to understand that I'm bound up with her in some fashion. Surely she has her own resident soul, but that isn't helping me one bit. I cannot make any sort of connection with her spirit, only a sensation that tells me much about her state of mind. All I can do is watch and wait for the powers that be to decide what is to become of me—and of this woman.

****

It's a rainy, windy day; as my sojourn observing this nameless woman continues, I've become aware that it's early spring and we're somewhere in Toronto. So I at least know I'm in familiar territory. The woman seems to be waiting for something to happen; she fidgets, paces—no, plods—around the flat, at least as far as she can in such tight spaces among her sad bits of furniture. For the first time since I've been drifting around here, there's a knock on the apartment door. At last! A visitor! Maybe something will finally happen to clear matters up. An older woman enters, encased in a hooded plastic raincoat still streaming with water. When she extracts herself from the raincoat, a whole lot of things instantly become clear to me.

Emerging from her wet clothing, Ellen Bruce embraces the younger woman.

"Hello, Perdita! Sorry I'm so late. It took forever to get a taxi and then the traffic was at a crawl. How are you feeling today, dear?"

And now I realize what I should have understood all along, why I ought to have known from the beginning who this young woman is, and why I'm here. Physical appearances and the realities of human bodies are seldom important to a soul, so we often don't catch on to things most humans would notice right away. Perdita's face, even though it's that of a young, pregnant woman, is virtually identical to a face that I grew to know very well. It's the face of a twenty-five-year-old Teddy McCoy. This can only be Teddy McCoy's daughter. Ellen's daughter, too.

Whoever the father of her as-yet-unborn child might be, he's obviously not on the scene. And I understand what is about to happen between me and that child. I'm not being offered any choice of hosts this time around. I have some unfinished business to attend to. It's unheard of for a soul to get a second chance at a human life—because each mortal only gets one go at it and there's no reason that souls should merit any special privileges. But this is about as close to a second chance as any soul is ever going to get. There's no other choice that I would consider, even if one were to be offered. All I can do is wait for the birth to take place; and, meanwhile, make it my business to learn all I can about Perdita and her infant. It cannot arrive soon enough; I mean to get on with this as soon as possible.

It may seem strange to you that souls have emotions; it doesn't seem to make sense that they should. But from all that I've told you until now, you've surely come to understand that it is so. I don't know if what I'm experiencing at this particular moment would be classified as joy; more likely happy anticipation, something akin to a kid about to open his Christmas presents; or perhaps more like an eager new graduate about to start his first job in his chosen field.

There is no chance that I'm going to let this child down!

****

Please be kind to the resident spirit that walks with you. Much is demanded of it, and it has been granted so little power with which to accomplish its tasks. Know that it wishes only your welfare. Learn to know it, to treasure the privilege of spending your moments in its company. It has been given a few fragments of wisdom that it seeks to share with you, if only you will open your mind to it. I understand that what I urge you to do is not easy; it requires an act of faith. Your mind has been trained from infancy not to believe in such foolishness. Those who say they hear voices are quickly hustled away for therapy; a danger to themselves—and perhaps to others. But I urge you toward courage.

To trust. To reach out. To thrive in spirit.

About the Author

JIM PUSKAS GREW UP IN a fractured family, which included relationships with several emotionally troubled family members. He has worked for many years in a variety of businesses involving major construction, steel fabrication, and execution of major contracts. Jim is officially retired but remains very active, taking a leading role in his immediate community. He is deeply engaged in volunteer work with Kiwanis, seeking to improve the lives of children, both locally and worldwide.

He reads very widely, often touching on matters of philosophy and metaphysics. Often, when reading, he's been prompted to think, "I could write something better than this!" He has enjoyed literature all his life and felt a need to tell a very unusual personal family story, which resulted in his first book, *Eastwind* (2015), available through AuthorHouse.

A member of both Kiwanis International and OACETT, Jim's other interests include gardening, travel, and a lifetime of learning new things and exploring new ideas. He lives in Ottawa with his wife Ruth, and a troublesome cat.

Printed in Canada